"I'd like to he...

"*Jah*. Unless there's ... , Levi said. Without thinking, he muttered, "Sadly, there's little hope of that."

Sadie lifted her eyebrows. "You don't want to go to the wedding, either?"

"Either? Does that mean *you* don't want to go? Why not?"

"You tell me why you don't want to go first."

Levi stalled. He couldn't express the real reason to Sadie. "Oh, er, it's that they last all day and it's hard on the *kinner* to miss their naps. They get cranky and then I worry they'll misbehave. Why don't you want to go?"

"I—I won't really know anyone there. I haven't even met the bride or groom yet."

Was that really the reason? "Then we should stick together," Levi replied. "That way, you can help with the *kinner* and I'll introduce you to everyone. How does that sound?"

"Not quite as *gut* as a blizzard, but I like it," Sadie said.

What Levi didn't know was if it was her smile or the hot chocolate warming his insides like that…

Carrie Lighte lives in Massachusetts next door to a Mennonite farming family, and she frequently spots deer, foxes, fisher cats, coyotes and turkeys in her backyard. Having enjoyed traveling to several Amish communities in the eastern United States, she looks forward to visiting settlements in the western states and in Canada. When she's not reading, writing or researching, Carrie likes to hike, kayak, bake and play word games.

Books by Carrie Lighte

Love Inspired

Amish of Serenity Ridge

Courting the Amish Nanny

Amish Country Courtships

Amish Triplets for Christmas
Anna's Forgotten Fiancé
An Amish Holiday Wedding
Minding the Amish Baby
Her New Amish Family
Her Amish Holiday Suitor

Visit the Author Profile page at Harlequin.com.

Courting the Amish Nanny

Carrie Lighte

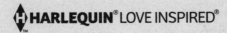

HARLEQUIN® LOVE INSPIRED®

LOVE INSPIRED BOOKS

Recycling programs
for this product may
not exist in your area.

ISBN-13: 978-1-335-47956-3

Courting the Amish Nanny

Copyright © 2019 by Carrie Lighte

Be careful for nothing; but in every thing by prayer and supplication with thanksgiving let your requests be made known unto God. And the peace of God, which passeth all understanding, shall keep your hearts and minds through Christ Jesus.
—*Philippians* 4:6–7

For my parents,
with gratitude for our Maine adventures

Chapter One

"If you go to Maine now, you'll miss *hochzich* season here," Sadie Dienner's stepmother, Cevilla, protested as she mixed water with flour to thicken the juice of a roast into gravy.

Jah, that's exactly my plan, Sadie thought. "I'm happy for Sarah and Rebekah, but we aren't exactly close friends," she said. "It's not as if I'm a *newehocker* in either *hochzich*."

She hardly expected to be asked to be a wedding attendant; the brides were each four years younger than twenty-five-year-old Sadie and she rarely saw them except at church. Sadie's closest friends had been married for years and she was painfully aware that once Sarah and Rebekah married their suitors this fall, she'd be the only single woman in Little Springs, Pennsylvania—with the exception of Elva Wyse, a ninety-two-year-old widow. And Elva had been married three times, so it wasn't as if she was considered a spinster.

"What about Harrison? Won't he be hurt if you don't attend his *hochzich* to Mary?"

Not nearly as hurt as I was when he told me he was

marrying her. The news had come as a shock to Sadie, who had long imagined marrying Harrison herself. In fact, he was the primary reason she wanted to flee Little Springs during wedding season. Not because she still entertained any romantic feelings toward him, but because her pride was wounded and the prospect of attending his wedding was too humiliating to bear.

Sadie cringed to remember what a fool she'd made of herself after Harrison and Mary's wedding was "published," or announced in church, a few weeks back in mid-October. The Old Order Amish youth in her district fiercely guarded their courtships, keeping them as secret as possible, so Sadie had assumed Harrison was interested in her and no one else. Come to find out, she was wrong on both counts.

"I didn't know you were courting someone from another district! All this time I thought—I thought you liked *me*," she'd wailed to him at work the Monday after his wedding was announced.

Perplexed, Harrison furrowed his brows. "I *do* like you. We're friends. I consider you a *gut* pal."

"A *pal*?" Sadie spit out the word.

"*Jah.* In some ways, I like spending time with you more than with Abe or Baker," Harrison had said with a grin, as if Sadie should have felt complimented she outranked his other buddies.

"But what about all the times you gave me a ride home from work?" Sadie sniffed, half enraged and half heartbroken, astonished he didn't return her romantic affections.

"What about it? We live in the same part of town. I'd do that much for anyone."

"Wh-what about the gifts?" The catch in Sadie's voice meant she was dangerously close to tears.

"Gifts?" Sadie could practically see the light dawning across his features. "Oh, you mean the Grischtdaag gift last year?"

"As well as the birthday present in March," Sadie reminded him, referencing the leather-covered diary Harrison had given her. The same diary in which she'd written all her dreams about him marrying her. "I thought those gifts meant something."

"They did. They were a reflection of how much my *familye* and I appreciate your work at the shop. Listen, Sadie, you're a valuable employee and—"

"Not anymore I'm not!" Sadie shot back. She already felt pitiful enough; she couldn't stand to listen to a consolation speech about the merits of her productivity at his family's furniture store when she'd hoped to hear declarations of love.

"What do you mean?"

"I mean I'm quitting," she declared. Her mouth made the decision before her mind thought it through, so she added, "You've said sales are waning and you've been struggling to pay two clerks. Sereta Miller is supporting her *eldre* and *suh*. She needs the job more than I do, so I volunteer to have my hours eliminated. Would you like to tell your *eldre* or do you want me to tell them?"

Harrison shook his head as if Sadie was speaking gibberish. "It's only a temporary lull. We expect business to pick up again in December. There's always a surge after Thanksgiving."

"By then, you'll be married and I'm sure your new wife will be glad to help out at the store," Sadie said with a shrug. At that point, she couldn't quite bring herself to acknowledge Mary by name.

That was nearly a month ago. Since then, Sadie had ruminated long and hard about how she had misinterpreted Harrison's gestures. She had convinced herself he was interested in her romantically but was too shy to ask to be her suitor. What a joke that was! He apparently hadn't been shy about asking Mary to become his wife.

Why isn't any man ever so enamored of me *that he can't wait to ask for* my *hand in marriage?* Sadie silently groused. This wasn't the first time a man had indicated, in so many words or actions, he thought of Sadie as a friend and nothing more. Something similar had happened with Albrecht Smoker and with Roy King, both of whom had actually walked out with her before deciding they weren't interested in continuing a courtship. Having grown up with seven brothers, Sadie wondered if there was something about her personality that caused men to feel comfortable around her but not drawn to her as a romantic prospect.

Either way, she regretted exposing her unrequited emotions to Harrison and she'd finished out the week at the furniture store feeling ridiculous in his presence. They'd stopped eating lunch together and she'd walked four miles home in the dark rather than accept a ride from him again. Not that he'd asked. He must have thought she was pathetic, because he'd gone as far out of his way to avoid her as she had to avoid him ever since. The way Sadie saw it, she'd be doing them both a favor by not attending his wedding.

"Harrison will have so many relatives there I doubt he'll even notice my absence," Sadie told her stepmother, retrieving a stack of plates from the cupboard.

"Besides, ever since I qu—I agreed to give my hours at the shop to Sereta, you've been telling me I need to find another job."

"*Jah*, but I meant a job in Little Springs."

"Your cousin's nephew needs help. And it's only temporary."

Cevilla chewed her lip and Sadie knew she'd made a good point. Her stepmother's cousin's nephew Levi was a widower with four-year-old twins. He owned a Christmas tree farm in Maine, where his mother had been minding the children for him, but she'd passed away in July. Apparently, the other nannies he'd employed hadn't worked out and now he was coming into his busiest season. After Christmas he was moving back to Indiana so his in-laws could help raise the twins, but until then, he was in desperate need of someone to care for them.

"I suppose that's true," Cevilla reluctantly admitted. "Besides, you're old enough to choose what you want to do."

"I want to go," Sadie firmly stated. "I really do."

Cevilla nodded but added, "Your *brieder* will miss having you here."

Sadie had three older brothers, who were married and lived locally in Pennsylvania, and four younger brothers at home, whom she doted on. "Tell them not to worry, I'll be back with their gifts just in time for Grischtdaag," she joked, but Cevilla was serious.

"*I'm* going to miss you. Maine is so far away," she said. "You've never even left Lancaster County."

That was because even when she'd had the opportunity, Sadie hadn't wanted to leave. But now she felt like she couldn't get far enough away. She set the last plate near her place at the table and crossed the kitchen to embrace Cevilla.

"I'll be back before you know it," she assured her stepmother. *And by then,* hochzich *season will be over and I'll be able to hold my head up in front of Harrison again.*

Levi Swarey firmly grasped the hands of his four-year-old twins, Elizabeth and David, as they skipped along beside him on the way to his mother's *daadi haus* across the lawn from his own home. Her death had hit him hard and he'd rarely been inside her house since she'd passed away in July. Afterward, the women from his church district had visited to collect her clothes for donation and give the place a good scrubbing down. They'd said they washed all the linens and stowed them away in the closet, so Levi figured that besides making up a bed there was little for him to do before Sadie moved in, but he wanted to double-check that she had everything she would need.

"I can smell Groossmammi," Elizabeth announced tearfully moments after they entered the empty house. "I want her to *kumme* back."

"Groossmammi can't *kumme* back. She's in heaven with the Lord and with Mamm," David said solemnly, repeating the explanation Levi had given the children countless times since his mother died.

Levi said, "*Jah,* and all three of them would want you to *wilkom* Sadie, so we need to make sure the *daadi haus* is cozy and clean. It looks pretty nice in here to me, what do you two think?"

"There's a big spiderweb in the corner." David

pointed to the wall above the thickly cushioned armchair. "Sadie might be afraid of spiders."

"That's not a spiderweb. It's a cow web," his sister corrected him.

"You're right, it is a *cob*web," Levi agreed. "I'll get the broom." He headed toward the kitchen. The broom wasn't hanging on its nail beside the refrigerator. Neither was it in the pantry, so he checked the bedroom, where he found it propped against the wall. He returned to the living room to discover David balanced on the back of the sofa. The boy jumped up and swiped at the cobweb with a doily he must have removed from an end table.

"Absatz!" Levi shouted for him to stop as he lunged forward and grabbed his son from the sofa. "How many times have I told you not to climb on furniture?"

David's lower lip quivered and tears bubbled in his eyes. "I was only trying to help *wilkom* Sadie, Daed."

"And he took his shoes off so he wouldn't get the couch dirty," Elizabeth defended him.

Levi picked David off the sofa and set him on the floor. Settling onto the cushion so he could be eye to eye with his son, Levi said, "I understand you wanted to help, but you could have fallen and broken your leg. And that would have broken my heart."

David's expression was one of anxiety as much as contrition and Levi knew he was overreacting. Again. He couldn't seem to help himself. As Levi sat there in his mother's house, it was almost as if he could hear her scolding him, *What happened to Leora was a* baremlich *thing,* suh, *but it's time you started trusting the Lord.*

He *did* trust the Lord. But trusting the Lord didn't relieve Levi of his responsibility to keep his children safe. He hadn't been able to protect their mother—on the contrary, it was his carelessness that had led to her death when the children were toddlers. He wasn't going to make that mistake with his children, no matter who thought he was overly protective.

And plenty of people did, which was why he'd lost the four nannies he'd had since his mother passed away. Levi's mother was the only person other than himself he trusted with their care, and he even caught himself looking over her shoulder, especially as the twins grew older and became more mobile.

"I know you're sorry," he told David. "But remember the rhyme I taught you?"

The twins duly chorused, "Keep safe and sound with both feet on the ground."

He insisted on this rule because of Leora's accident three years ago. She had been cleaning the windows when she must have lost her balance. After falling and cracking her skull on the stone hearth behind her, she'd suffered a subarachnoid hemorrhage and died. Although Levi's mother had come to live in the *daadi haus* by the time, on that particular day she had been out of town. Leora and the children had been home alone. But the Lord had been merciful; a neighbor happened to stop by for tea and discovered Leora sprawled across the floor, a kettle screaming from the stove and the twins wailing in their cribs. Even now it horrified Levi to consider what else might have happened if no one had come by before then. He'd never forgiven himself for failing to return Leora's stepladder to its spot in the pantry. He had used it the day before when he was trimming dead limbs from the apple tree at the back of the house and then he'd forgotten it there. Leora must not have wanted to leave the babies while they were napping, so instead of fetching the solid stepladder, she'd stood on a chair from the kitchen. Borrowing household items and not returning them was one of Levi's habits that had nettled his wife to no end, but until then, he had never imagined his carelessness would result in tragedy. What kind of spouse was so thoughtless about his wife's needs? Levi came to believe he hadn't deserved to be a husband, and sometimes he wondered why the Lord had entrusted him with children. But as long as they were his, he would do everything he could to keep them safe.

The twins might not have understood the origins of the rule about keeping their feet firmly planted, but they understood they were meant to obey it. "I won't do it again, Daed," David promised.

"How about if you and Elizabeth take turns sweeping and I'll open the windows to air out Groossmammi's place a little?"

"So her smell doesn't make us sad anymore?" Elizabeth wondered.

If only it were that simple. Levi swallowed the lump in his throat. His children had lost so much at such a young age. They'd hardly known their mother, their beloved grandmother had died of congestive heart failure, and although they didn't know it yet, they were about to have to bid their home and community goodbye, too.

Given his mother's death and the lack of suitable nannies in the area, Levi had realized he had little choice but to move back to Indiana, where Leora's parents would help provide Elizabeth and David with the kind of stability and long-term care they needed. As grateful as he was for their help, Levi was concerned about how difficult the relocation would be for the children—and he had his own qualms about moving in with Leora's family, as well. He hadn't been especially close to his wife's parents when she was alive, and after she passed on, Levi sensed they blamed him nearly as much as he blamed himself for her death. Not that he had ever told them—or anyone—about his part in his wife's accident, but Leora's parents had been terribly nervous when he and their daughter had ventured off to Maine. After Leora died, Levi imagined they felt their fears had been justified.

Nevertheless, he'd begun making all the necessary relocation preparations, and he already had two prospective buyers who were very interested in the house and farm. As for employment in Indiana, he planned to take a job in an RV factory or work construction again. But first things first: Levi had to make it through Christmas season. After seven years, the trees were finally ready to harvest. If all went well and sales were what he expected them to be, Levi would have enough money to repay the loan on the land he and Leora had bought back when they were young newlyweds in love and thought they had their entire lives together spread out before them.

"Jah." Levi finally answered his daughter's question, but he could have been talking to himself. "It's better not to be reminded of things that make us sad. If we open the windows, the scent of the trees will waft inside."

"Then the *haus* will smell like Grischtdaag. And Grischtdaag is a happy smell," Elizabeth said.

"Jah," David agreed. "That's because Grischtdaag is when *wunderbaar* things happen, isn't it, Daed?"

In response, Levi smiled wanly and tousled his son's hair. Holidays weren't the same after Leora had died.

Since his mother had also passed on, Levi didn't even know how they'd spend Thanksgiving Day. The thought of celebrating Christmas felt overwhelming to him. He'd be so busy selling trees beforehand and then selling the house shortly afterward he felt like he wouldn't have any time for festivities. But knowing the children were looking forward to the holidays gave him a boost of motivation. *We'll have joy again in our* haus *before we move if it's the last thing we do*, he decided.

Sadie leaned her head against the window of the van. Although traveling by vehicle made her nauseated, she knew the older *Englisch* couple who'd transported members of her district for years were cautious drivers, and she shifted into a more relaxing position.

It was a long trip from Little Springs, Pennsylvania, to Serenity Ridge, Maine. She'd begun the day excited to see sights she'd only read about—the scenic Pocono Mountains and Hudson River; cities like Allentown, Hartford and Worcester; and *Englisch* neighborhoods with houses spaced so close together it seemed the residents could stick their hands out their windows and touch each other's fingertips. It was dusk by the time the van crossed the bridge linking Maine and New Hampshire, and the closer they got to their final destination, the more densely forested the land became. *No wonder they nicknamed this the Pine Tree State*, she thought.

That was one of the few facts Sadie knew about Maine. As for the Amish community in Serenity Ridge, it was one of a handful of settlements that had been established in Maine in the past two or three decades. The families there hailed from places as disparate as Canada, Pennsylvania, Ohio, Indiana, Missouri and Tennessee.

Some were drawn to the area because the land was less expensive than in their home states; others came in pursuit of new opportunities or to escape the Amish tourism industry. The Maine settlements were still growing, and from what Sadie heard, Serenity Ridge only had about fifteen small Amish families in residence.

That will be gut. The fewer people, the less chance of there being any hochzichen *while I'm there*, she thought.

For the umpteenth time, Sadie inwardly chastised herself for acting so rashly and quitting her job. Harrison probably thought he'd really broken her heart, when actually she was over him within a week. *That's because I wasn't truly in love with Harrison*, she'd written in her diary when the realization struck her. *I was infatuated with infatuation. From now on, I'm putting those notions out of my head. Romance isn't everything after all.* Confident a change of scenery would reinforce her new perspective, Sadie pushed any lingering embarrassment from her mind and quietly hummed the rest of the way to Serenity Ridge.

Once they arrived at the *daadi haus*, the driver carried her luggage to the porch and wished her the best. Sadie pushed open the door, which Levi had indicated would be unlocked when he left the address and a brief voice mail on the machine at the phone shanty.

He must have turned up the gas heat for her, because the kitchen was toasty and so was the small living room. The *daadi haus* also contained a bathroom and two cozy bedrooms. To Sadie's surprise, her host had even made both beds up and set extra quilts at the foot of each one. *What a thoughtful thing to do. He must have known I'd be exhausted.* Deciding there'd be time enough for unpacking before she went to Levi's house to meet him and the twins tomorrow, Sadie fell into bed.

Her deep sleep was punctuated only by a morning dream about Christmas trees that was so real it seemed as if she was woken by their fragrance. But no, it was a rapping on the door that forced her to open her eyes and jump out of bed. It took a moment for her to recognize her surroundings before she cloaked her shoulders in a quilt and shuffled to the mudroom.

"Guder mariye." The rangy man who greeted her had a slightly crooked nose, a shock of dark hair and thick eyebrows framing his doleful green eyes. But it was his facial hair that really caught Sadie's attention; not only was he sporting the usual Amish beard men wore after marrying, but he had a neatly trimmed mustache, too.

Suddenly remembering her manners, she replied, *"Guder mariye."*

He must have noticed her gaze, because he pointed to his face and said, "Here in Maine, we do things a little differently. Mustaches aren't forbidden. They're not required, either."

Sadie was so caught off guard by his forthrightness and so embarrassed he'd noticed her staring that she pulled back and stuttered, "I—I—"

Fortunately, the children interrupted. "My name is Elizabeth," lisped the chubby girl with a missing tooth.

"I'm David," the boy piped up. He was the spitting image of his father, although his nose was smaller and straight.

"I'm four years old. Almost five," Elizabeth proudly announced.

"Me, too," David informed Sadie, as if she wasn't aware they were twins.

Smiling, she replied, "*Guder mariye.* I'm Sadie Dienner."

"*Denki* for coming to help us on such short notice," Levi said. "I'm Levi, by the way."

"Hello, Levi. It's my pleasure to be here. Not that I'm glad about the circumstances, of course, but I'm... I'm—" Sadie stopped herself midsentence. She was babbling and probably blushing, too.

Levi acted as if she hadn't misspoken. "Sorry to wake you so early after your long trip, but we brought you *millich* and *oier*. And we thought you'd want to ride to church with us. It's almost time to leave, so while you're, um, getting dressed, we'll bring the buggy around front."

Back in Little Springs, today would have been an off-Sunday, meaning Amish families worshipped in their own homes instead of gathering as a group at a designated house. But not all districts followed the same schedule. Sadie pushed her long, light brown ringlets over her shoulder, suddenly aware she wasn't wearing a prayer *kapp*, and accepted the basket with one hand while still clutching the blanket tight around her with the other.

"*Denki.* I'll be ready in just a few minutes." Before closing the door with her foot she stole another glance at the hair above Levi's lip. Although it took a moment to grow accustomed to the sight of it, she had to admit it was becoming to him.

The old Sadie might have been tempted to imagine a courtship with him, but the new Sadie isn't going to give it a second thought, she resolutely decided.

* * *

Levi was expecting a younger woman, maybe seventeen or eighteen at most. Until this morning, he and Sadie hadn't actually spoken. They'd only left a couple of sparsely detailed messages on the machines at each other's phone shanties. All Levi knew was Sadie was the stepdaughter of a distant relative, that she'd helped care for her four younger siblings and that she was willing to come to Maine right away. He'd never thought to ask how old she was. Not that it mattered; it was just that he was surprised someone her age wasn't married and didn't have a family of her own.

Maybe she's widowed, too, he mused but quickly dismissed the idea. There was nothing about her expression suggesting the shadow of grief. Quite the opposite: her eyes were as blue as a cloudless sky and her complexion was just as sunny. If anything, she seemed a bit self-conscious; perhaps because she'd just woken and her hair was loose and mussed from sleep. Even so, her lips were pert with a breezy smile. Vaguely recalling when Leora used to appear as luminous as that, Levi sighed.

"Kumme," he called to the children and headed to the stable, where the pair of them stayed outside and sat on the stone wall. He required them to keep a safe distance whenever he was hitching or unhitching the horse and buggy. Once finished, he signaled them to approach and they climbed into the back seat so there'd be room for Sadie—who joined them just then—to sit up front with Levi.

"Look at all the pine trees!" she exclaimed as they traversed the long straight road that cut across town. "I could only see their outlines last night. They seem even bigger in the daylight."

"Don't you have pine trees where you come from?" Elizabeth asked.

"Not nearly as many as you have here. I've never been out of Lancaster County, so it's fun to see new sights."

"Later in the week I can take you to the *Englisch* supermarket," Levi offered. "The library and post office, too. Since we're still a young settlement, we don't have as many Amish businesses as you probably have in Little Springs."

"Do the Englischers gawk at you when you're in town?"

"*Neh*, not at this time of year. Most of them are year-round residents and they're used to us by now. They've been *wunderbaar* about accepting us into the community but also respecting our differences. Summer is a different story, though, because that's when tourists *kumme* to vacation on Serenity Ridge Lake. To them we're a novelty. Or part of the scenery—I've been photographed too many times to count."

Sadie clicked her tongue sympathetically. Then she pointed to a house. "There's another one!"

"Another what?"

"A green roof. They're everywhere."

"*Jah*, they're made of metal," Levi said, amused by her observation. He'd been here long enough that he didn't notice the differences between Maine and his home state anymore. "Metal roofing is very popular here because it's durable and energy efficient. Plus, it keeps ice dams from forming, which is important during our harsh winters. One of our district members, Colin Blank, owns a metal roofing company and he can hardly keep up with the demand."

Sadie nodded, clearly taking it all in. She was quiet until they turned onto the dirt road and Levi announced their destination was at the top of the hill. "What a strange-looking *haus*," she remarked. "Who lives here?"

"No one." Levi chuckled. Her bewilderment was winsome. "It's a church building."

"You worship in a building instead of a home?" Sadie asked so incredulously it sounded as if she was accusing them of something scandalous.

"*Jah.* The settlement in Unity does, too. It's a rarity, but it makes sense for us since we're so spread out and this is the most central location."

"Wow. Is there anything else I should know about Amish life in Maine?"

"Hmm… Well, on Thanksgiving we eat smoked moose instead of turkey," Levi teased.

Sadie's eyebrows shot up. "Really?"

Levi felt guilty about the alarmed look on her face. "*Neh.* I was only kidding. We have turkey and all the usual fixings."

"Have you ever encountered a moose?"

"*Neh.* Fortunately. If they feel threatened, they can be very dangerous creatures."

"You should always give them lots of space," Elizabeth advised from the back seat.

"And never get in between a *mamm* moose and its calf," David warned. "Because the *mamm* might charge."

"I'll remember that," Sadie said. "Although I'm a pretty fast runner, so if it charged it would probably *moose* me."

David and Elizabeth cracked up, but Levi had to bite his tongue to keep from telling Sadie it wasn't a joking matter. He hoped she wasn't going to be glib about the rules he had for the children's safety or reckless about their care, the way the other nannies had been. *Overbearing*, one of them had called him in response to his reminders. But what did she know about the responsibilities involved in raising children? She was practically a child herself.

At least Sadie's older than the other meed *were*, he thought. But older didn't necessarily mean wiser. Suddenly, he was struck by a worrisome thought: Why had someone Sadie's age traveled all this way to take a job usually reserved for teenage girls? She'd been so highly recommended by his uncle that Levi hadn't thought to ask why she was willing to come to Maine—during Christmas season, no less! Levi was only distantly related to Cevilla, so it wasn't as if Sadie was fulfilling a familial obligation. Maybe she couldn't find employment in Pennsylvania—or worse, she'd had a job but was fired.

The other possibilities that occupied Levi's mind throughout the church service were equally unsettling. As the congregation rose to sing the closing hymn, Levi decided the only way to know if Sadie was a good nanny would be to keep an even closer watch on her than he had on the others. And somehow, he was going to have to accomplish that feat without offending her with his scrutiny.

Dear Lord, give me wisdom and tact, he silently prayed. *And if I've made a mistake by hiring Sadie, please show me before any harm befalls my precious* kinner.

Chapter Two

Although there were fewer families present and church was held in a building instead of a house—and although half of the men wearing beards also wore mustaches—the worship service in Serenity Ridge was very similar to the services Sadie was accustomed to in Little Springs and she felt right at home. Especially because afterward the women greeted her warmly as she helped them prepare the standard after-church lunch of peanut butter, bread, cold cuts, cheese, pickled beets and chow-chow in the little kitchen in the basement.

A svelte, energetic blonde woman about five or six years older than Sadie introduced herself as Maria Beiler, one of Levi's seasonal employees. She said she'd be making wreaths and working the cash register at the farm. "It's so *gut* of you to *kumme* all the way from Pennsylvania. I don't know what Levi would have done if you hadn't arrived to watch the *kinner*."

"I suppose it's difficult to find a nanny in such a small district," Sadie replied modestly.

"Not nearly as difficult as *keeping* one," Maria mumbled.

"What do you mean?" Sadie asked, but Maria had whisked a basket of bread from the counter and was already on her way to the gathering room. Her curiosity piqued, Sadie wondered what could be so difficult about retaining a nanny to mind these children. From what she could tell so far, David and Elizabeth were exceptionally well behaved and sweet, if a little timid.

Then it occurred to her Levi might be the one who presented a challenge. He did seem a bit uptight, lacking the sense of humor to laugh at her corny moose joke. But that hardly qualified as a personality flaw and it didn't overshadow his thoughtfulness in warming up the *daadi haus* for her or bringing her milk and eggs. Since Sadie knew she wasn't the best judge of men's characters, she decided to let Maria's remark slide. After all, this was a short-term position, and as far as Sadie was concerned, it didn't matter if the children were incorrigible or Levi was a two-headed monster; she could tolerate anything if it meant avoiding wedding season in Little Springs.

After lunch the women sent Sadie home carrying a canvas bag bulging with plastic containers of leftovers, since she hadn't been to the supermarket yet and didn't have anything in her cupboards to snack on. She offered to share the food with Levi and the children at supper, but Levi insisted she enjoy it at leisure by herself. "The Sabbath is a day of rest and you've had a long trip. You'll be preparing meals for us soon enough."

Although Sadie appreciated his consideration, she wasn't used to spending Sunday afternoon and evening all alone, and by Monday morning she was so antsy to hear the sound of another person's voice, she showed up at Levi's house half an hour early.

"Who is it?" Elizabeth squeaked from the other side of the door.

"It's me, Sadie," she answered, wondering who else the child thought could be arriving at that hour. She heard a bolt sliding from its place—in Little Springs, the Amish never locked their houses when they were at home—before the door swung open.

"Guder mariye," the twins said in unison.

"Guder mariye," Sadie replied as she made her way into the mudroom. After taking off her coat and shoes and continuing through to the kitchen, she remarked, "Look at you, both dressed already. Have you eaten breakfast, too?"

"Neh, Daed said if we waited maybe you'd make us oatmeal 'cause when he makes it it's as thick as cement."

Sadie laughed. "I'm happy to make oatmeal. But where is your *daed*? Out milking the cow?"

"Neh," Levi answered as he entered the room. His face was rosy as if it had been freshly scrubbed, and Sadie noticed droplets of water sparkling from the corners of his mustache. She quickly refocused to meet his eyes. He added, "I wouldn't leave the *kinner* here alone. I hope you wouldn't, either."

Sadie was puzzled. Most Amish children Elizabeth and David's age could be trusted to behave if their parents momentarily stepped outside to milk the cow or hang the laundry. What was it about the twins that gave Levi pause about leaving them unsupervised? If Sadie didn't figure it out by herself soon, she'd ask him later in private. "Of course I wouldn't. We'll stick together like glue." Then she jested, "Or like cement."

Levi cocked his head when the children giggled. Then he got it. "Aha, my *kinner* must have told you about my cooking." Laughing at his own expense, he proved he wasn't humorless after all.

"Cooking is my responsibility now," Sadie said, since she'd agreed to make meals for the Swarey family. She was invited to eat with them as a perk, in addition to her salary. "I'll have breakfast ready by the time you return from the barn. Maybe Elizabeth wants to help me make it."

Elizabeth's eyes glistened. *"Jah—"* she said before Levi cut her off.

"Neh, she's too young to operate the stove. She can *kumme* with David and me to the barn."

Seeing Elizabeth's shoulders sag, Sadie opened her mouth to inform Levi she had no intention of allowing Elizabeth turn on the gas, but that didn't mean the girl couldn't assist in the kitchen. Then she figured Levi knew more about his daughter's abilities than Sadie, so she helped Elizabeth into her coat, hat and mittens while Levi did the same for David.

By the time the trio returned from milking the cow and collecting eggs, breakfast was on the table. In between swallowing spoonfuls of oatmeal, Levi explained, "Even though it's only the sixteenth of November, we're harvesting the first trees this week so we can ship them to our *Englisch* vendors who open their lots the day after Thanksgiving. I've also got a few dozen customers who ordered early deliveries of oversize trees for their places of business. You know, local restaurants and shops. A dentist's office. A couple of churches, too."

Sadie appreciated hearing about his job. She'd grown up on a farm, but they primarily grew corn and wheat; she had no idea what was involved in harvesting Christmas trees. "How many people do you have on your crew besides Maria Beiler?"

"This week it's me and four young men from our district. Plus two *Englisch* truck drivers, who will help bale and load, too. After Thanksgiving we'll have fewer deliveries. For the most part customers will cut and carry the trees themselves, or else we'll bag and burlap the live ones, so I'll reassign staff to manage all of that," Levi said. He stopped to guzzle down the rest of his juice. "Which reminds me, my brother-in-law, Otto, will be arriving the Saturday after Thanksgiving to help. I hope you don't mind cooking for him, too?"

"That's fine. I'm used to preparing meals for a group of *hungerich* men—I have seven *brieder*," Sadie said before asking what made him decide to grow Christmas trees. It seemed an odd choice of crops, considering most Amish people didn't allow Christmas trees in their own houses.

"The Englischer who sold us the acreage had already planted the seedlings about three years before we arrived. Then his parents had some health issues, so he relocated to Portland to care for them. My wife and I originally planned to clear the land and grow potatoes, but the previous owner had already invested so much into the trees we ended up changing our minds. All told, it's taken over ten years for the trees to be ready to sell. In the meantime, I've also been working for Colin—the man I told you about—who owns a roofing company, so I'd have a steady income until we could turn a profit."

"Did you live on a farm in Indiana, too?"

"*Neh*. I worked construction. In fact, that's why Leora—my wife… That's why she wanted to move to Maine in the first place. We couldn't afford to buy farmland in Indiana and it was her dream to raise our *kinner* in the countryside…" Levi's voice wavered and he dragged a napkin across his mouth.

Sadie regretted that she'd stirred a painful memory and tried to console him. "I'm sure your wife would be pleased you're fulfilling her dream for the *kinner*." But her comment seemed to upset Levi even more.

He pushed his chair from the table and scowled. "I've got a busy day ahead of me, so I don't have time for any more chitchat."

Embarrassed by his brusque dismissal, Sadie rose to her feet, too. "Then I won't keep you. I'm sure the *kinner* know what their chores are and can help me find whatever I need in the house, although we'll probably spend time outdoors, too."

"*Neh*, I don't want you taking Elizabeth and David outside."

Sadie was baffled as to why Levi expected them to stay inside; the weather was cloudy and cold, but she'd take care to dress them warmly. Were they recovering from a recent illness and in need of rest? Or perhaps a wild animal had been roaming the property and Levi didn't want to frighten the children by mentioning it in front of them. While their father was donning his outerwear, Sadie directed David and Elizabeth to go upstairs and make their beds so she could ask Levi in private why they weren't allowed outside.

He answered, "There will be trucks on-site today and I don't want them running along the driveway or even playing in the yard until I've had a chance to show you around the property. I need to point out places to avoid. There's a shallow little pond at the bottom of the hill on the opposite side of the barn, for example."

Puzzled, Sadie quipped, "I wasn't planning to take them swimming. Not in this weather anyway." But when Levi glowered and pushed his hat onto his head, she cleared her throat and added, "We'll stay on this side of the driveway and keep far away from the trucks, I promise."

"I said I didn't want them going outside yet!" he snapped. "Those are my rules for my *kinner* and if you have a problem following them, perhaps you made a mistake by coming here."

Sadie saw red. *I'm not the one who has a problem*, she thought, but she didn't say it. She had already quit one job impetuously; she wasn't going to quit this one, too. At least, not without considering it carefully. The thought of sitting through Harrison's wedding made her wince, but she wasn't sure she could work for someone as unreasonable as Levi, either.

"You're right. Perhaps I did make a mistake by coming here," she replied evenly. "I'll have to give it more thought."

Levi pulled his chin back as if surprised. "You do that, then," he said. "But before I go, I'd like you to look this over. It lists what's expected of David and Elizabeth, as well as what they're not allowed to do."

He went and retrieved a sheet of paper from on top of the fridge and handed it to Sadie and then looked over her shoulder as she read it. *The children are not allowed to get too close to the woodstove. The children cannot handle knives. They mustn't climb on furniture.* The list continued on and on. Scanning it, Sadie doubted even the least experienced nanny would need such detailed guidelines to care for Elizabeth and David. Nor did she consider all the rules to be necessary, but she held her tongue.

"Any questions?" he asked when she glanced up.

"*Neh*, no questions."

"*Gut.* I'll stop by in an hour or two."

If he's so pressed for time, why would he bother coming back in an hour? "Oh, there's no need to disrupt your work," Sadie suggested. "We'll be fine until you return for lunch. When would you like to eat?"

"One o'clock," he replied so gruffly it confirmed Sadie's suspicion he was the reason the other nannies had quit.

Before leaving the house, Levi called David and Elizabeth back downstairs. He placed a hand on each of his children's heads, the way he always did before he left them for a length of time. After silently praying for their safety, he removed his hands and gave them each a kiss on the cheek. *"Ich leibe dich,"* he said and the twins told him they loved him, too.

On the porch he pushed his fingers into his gloves. Although the worst of his grief had subsided over the years, talking about Leora's dream to live on a farm had brought up sorrowful emotions. Levi regretted she didn't live to see the tree harvest finally coming to fruition. His wife believed farming was doing God's work and she envisioned the two of them as pioneers, setting out for Maine on their own. Even though she missed Indiana and her family and experienced terrible morning sickness with the twins, Leora had never complained because she said their move was going to be worth it.

Levi knew she would have been devastated he and the children were leaving Maine. But what else could he do? He'd already lost two nannies from his district, one from nearby Unity and one from Smyrna, in the northern part of the state, who had been visiting her cousins in Serenity Ridge. He doubted there were any other Amish nannies he'd find remotely suitable left in Maine, and if Sadie was any indication, Pennsylvania wasn't that promising, either.

Judging from the conversation he'd just had with her, she wasn't going to work out. Which was disappointing—Elizabeth and David had taken an instant liking to her; in contrast with the other nannies, Sadie had shown a genuine interest in them, too. Levi had prayed for guidance. If Sadie refused to honor his instructions or chose to quit, that was as much clarity as he could ask for in regard to whether he'd made a mistake by hiring her. And when it came to his children's well-being, it was better to know sooner rather than later if she was a suitable match.

The sound of a truck clattering up the gravel road jarred Levi from his thoughts. Signaling the driver, Scott, to stop, he crossed the lawn to the barn, which was located on the opposite side of his house from the *daadi haus.* Halfway in between his house and the barn was a small workshop. Last week he'd rearranged his tools and workbenches to create an area where Maria could make wreaths. Beginning the day after Thanksgiving, the workshop would also serve as a place for her to ring up sales when the farm opened to the public. But Levi didn't expect Maria to arrive until nine o'clock, so he continued toward the barn, where he stored the portable baler, the machine used to shake the needles from the trees and the chain and handsaws.

By the time he and Scott loaded the equipment onto the truck bed, the rest of the crew had arrived. Levi spent the next couple of hours explaining the tagging system, showing the young men around the sixteen-acre farm, and demonstrating how to operate the machinery and palletize the trees for shipment, the way he'd learned from working at a tree farm the previous year. The guys groaned when he reminded them they were required to wear goggles and ear protection whenever they used the chain saws, so he delivered a stern lecture on injury prevention.

He intended to supervise their work until he was confident they knew what they were doing and would do it safely, but Walker Huyard, a young Amish man who was employed by a tree service company during the warmer months, pulled him aside. "A word to the wise is sufficient," he said. "You've got an experienced crew here."

"What do you mean?"

Walker returned his question with a question. "Does Colin Blank watch you like a hawk or nag you like a schoolmarm when you're roofing for him?"

Levi got his point; on occasion Colin *was* overbearing, much to the consternation of his employees. Clapping Walker on the shoulder, he said, "You're right. I'll leave you guys to it. I'm going to take a break and I'll be back by ten thirty—to help, not to harp on you."

He returned to the house to discover the kitchen empty, but laughter spilled from the living room, where Elizabeth and David snuggled against Sadie on the sofa. They were so enraptured by whatever she was saying they didn't immediately notice his arrival. *I don't know if the* kinner *could handle the upheaval of another nanny leaving. Especially not Sadie.* More to the point, he had no idea who he'd get for a replacement.

Pausing silently at the threshold of the room, he studied her animated gestures; something about the artful way she moved her hands reminded him of Leora and he realized his wife had been Sadie's age when her life was cut short.

Sadie suddenly noticed his presence. "Can I help you?" she asked dryly.

"*Neh*, I'm just checking up on you." That sounded wrong. "I mean, checking *in* on you. To make sure there's nothing you need, that is."

"*Denki*, we're all set." Her tone remained politely formal.

"Sadie's telling us stories about her *brieder*," Elizabeth said.

"One time they used a pulley and a clothesline to fly from the loft of the barn to a tree on the other side of the fence!" David exclaimed.

"Her *bruder* Joseph got stuck halfway across and he was too scared to let go, so Sadie's other *brieder* had to reel him back like a fish," Elizabeth recited.

Despite his intention to smooth things over with Sadie, Levi had been cautioning his children for so long it was second nature to him to blurt out, "That sounds very dangerous. I imagine they gave Sadie's *mamm* and *daed* a fright and they probably received a harsh punishment."

"*Neh*, my *eldre* didn't find out until afterward, when it was clear Joseph was okay. My *daed* was impressed by the ingenuity and durability of their invention. Besides, we positioned our trampoline near the end of the line so we could let go before we hit the tree. It was a lot safer than jumping out of the loft into a pile of straw the way we usually did," Sadie said with a laugh.

"Her *brieder* were afraid to try it, but Sadie went first and then they all wanted a turn," Elizabeth interjected.

Levi pointed his finger at his daughter. "If I ever saw you dangling from a rope in the air, I'd be very, very upset." As Elizabeth's expression changed from jubilant to ashamed, Levi realized how punitive he must have sounded, when what he meant to express was how disturbed he'd be if she was ever in such a dangerous position. Trying to assure his daughter she wasn't being scolded, he said, "But I don't have to worry about that because you're not a tomboy."

"Not yet, she isn't," Sadie countered. "She's too young to determine what kind of personality or interests she'll develop. But just because she's a *maedel* doesn't mean she shouldn't run and climb and jump and explore the outdoors. Physical exercise is *gut* for children, both *buwe* and *meed*."

As Sadie spoke, her eyes flashed a warning Levi was walking on thin ice. "I only meant it would have alarmed me if Elizabeth—or David, for that matter— had gotten stuck the way Joseph did. I didn't mean there's anything wrong with a girl being active," he tried to explain. "My Leora was one of the most adventurous women I've ever known. I'll be pleased if Elizabeth takes after her *mamm* in that way—but that'll be when she's older and can judge for herself whether or not a risk is worth taking. Until then, she needs the guidance of responsible adults."

Sadie didn't look at all appeased. She blinked twice before freeing her arms from the children's grasp and standing up. "You mentioned how much work you have to get done today, so you probably want to return to it now. And I need to begin preparing lunch."

I'm still *on thin ice*, Levi thought. Not wanting to push her, he figured he could go back to reminding the children about their safety rules tonight. Right now he sensed if he didn't back off, Sadie would decide to pack her bags that evening. "Don't worry about tidying the kitchen or making hot meals for lunch. Sandwiches are fine. The most important thing is the *kinner* are well cared for. And you're right, a little exercise is *gut* for them. If the rain lets up, maybe you can take them for a walk to the barn and back."

Did he imagine it or did Sadie roll her eyes before glancing at David and Elizabeth and asking, "What do you think, *kinner*? Can you make it all the way to the barn and back?"

Unsure if she was teasing the children or taking a swipe at him, Levi joked, "If they can't, I'll swing by on the clothesline and pick them up."

The children laughed, but Sadie's expression remained unreadable. "I'll see you at lunchtime, then," he muttered awkwardly, exiting the house as quickly as his feet could carry him.

If Levi thought his comment about sandwiches being acceptable to him or his concession in allowing her to take the children outside was going to win Sadie over, he had another think coming. *If the rain lets up? It's barely drizzling*, Sadie fumed as she squared the potatoes for stew. She'd never encountered an Amish father—especially one who lived on a farm—who didn't fully expect his children to play and do their chores outside in weather far worse than this. Was this one of the differences between the Amish in Maine and the Amish in Pennsylvania, or was it simply one of Levi's quirks?

And what exactly did he mean about Elizabeth not being a tomboy? Sadie resented the word that had often been used to describe her, too. Which wasn't to say she didn't relish being every bit as agile, strong and intrepid as her brothers. But like the word *pal*, the word *tomboy* had negative connotations when a man used it to describe a woman. To Sadie it indicated he thought she didn't also have the feminine interests and qualities that men admired and appreciated in a woman.

She covered the pot and set it on the stove to simmer. "What do I care what Levi thinks of me as a woman anyway?" she muttered. She wasn't even sure if she was going to stay there.

"Who are you talking to?" David was suddenly at her elbow.

"Oh, sometimes I think out loud," she admitted. "So, what did you and your *schweschder* usually do with your *groossmammi* in the mornings once your chores were done?"

"Groossmammi read to us."

"Or we played board games or colored," Elizabeth piped up as she entered the room.

"I see," Sadie said. She wondered whether their sedentary activities were because their grandmother had been ill and didn't have a lot of energy, or because of Levi's restrictions. "The sun is peeking out from the clouds, so let's take that walk to the barn now."

The children scurried to the mudroom, where Sadie helped them into their boots, coats, mittens and hats. As soon as they stepped outside, Elizabeth and David simultaneously slid their hands into Sadie's. Although she was happy to receive the gesture as a sign of affection, she was surprised they didn't want to run freely, the way most children did after being cooped indoors for any length of time.

"Let's make a dash for it!" she urged and began sprinting across the yard toward the barn. But the children couldn't keep up and she didn't want to tug too hard on their arms, so she slowed to a casual stroll. As they approached the workshop she noticed a lamp burning and asked the children if they thought their father was inside. *If I see him again right now, I might not be able to censor myself.*

David answered, "*Neh*, that's where Maria Beiler makes wreaths."

Another woman to talk to; that was just what Sadie needed at the moment to take the edge off her unpleasant interaction with Levi. "Let's stop in and say hello." As soon as she opened the door, the scent of balsam filled her nostrils.

"What a *wunderbaar* surprise—*wilkom*!" Maria greeted them. "Would you like a demonstration of my one-woman wreath-making workshop in action?"

She proceeded to show them how she collected boughs from the bin the crew had filled outside the door. Then she cut the trimmings into a suitable size and arranged them neatly around a specially designed wire ring. Using a foot-pedaled machine, she clamped the prongs on the ring, securing the boughs into place. Finally, she fastened a bright red or gold ribbon on the wreath and then carefully hung it from a peg on a large portable rack.

"As you can see, I'm running out of bows," she said.

"I like to make them at home ahead of time but since yesterday was the Sabbath, I'm falling behind."

"I can tie a few bows into shape so you can keep assembling the other parts," Sadie volunteered.

"*Denki*, but this is my job. You've got your hands full enough yourself."

"Please," Sadie pleaded.

Maria smiled knowingly. "Do you have a case of cabin fever already?" she asked. Without waiting for an answer, she handed Sadie a spool of ribbon, and to the children's delight, she announced she needed their help on a special project. She supplied them with pre-cut lengths of red and green cord, as well as a glue stick to share, before leading them to a crate filled with thin slices of tree trunks. She explained how to glue the cord onto the trunk slices, transforming them into ornaments the customers' children could take for free to decorate their trees at home.

As Maria was setting up their workbench, Sadie deftly fashioned the stiff ribbon into fat loops until she formed a half-dozen bows and then stopped to affix one on each wreath from the pile. When she finished, she repeated the process as quickly as she could in order to keep up with Maria.

Once their work fell into a steady rhythm, Maria asked, "So, are you…getting on all right at the *haus*?"

"*Jah,*" Sadie answered carefully. "Although I'm discovering parents do things a little differently in Maine than in Pennsylvania."

"Ha!" Maria uttered. When the children looked her way, she lowered her voice to confide, "The parenting differences you've noticed have nothing to do with Maine."

"So were those, uh, *differences* the reason the other two nannies left?"

"Two? There were *four* nannies before you, and *jah*, that's exactly why they left," Maria whispered. "To be fair, Levi wasn't always like this. He used to be fairly easygoing. But after his wife died, he became really controlling."

Sadie felt guilty for gossiping, but she wanted to know. "How did his wife die?"

"She fell off a chair cleaning a window and hit her head. A neighbor found her and called an ambulance, but she was already gone," Maria lamented and Sadie's eyes filled. "I think Levi's afraid something like that might happen to his *kinner*, too, and that's why he's overly protective. His *mamm* was the only person he trusted to take care of them. Ever since she died and he's had to rely on nannies, he's become even more cautious. I know it must be difficult to tolerate. That's one of the reasons I'm working in the shop instead of watching the *kinner* myself. But..."

"But it helps to know why he is the way he is," Sadie finished her sentence. "*Denki* for sharing that. It gives me a different outlook."

"*Gut*, because I was close friends with Leora and I'm still very fond of Levi. I'd hate for him to lose you, too—"

"Hey, I was using that!" Elizabeth scolded her brother, who hugged the glue stick to his chest so she couldn't take it.

Her conversation with Maria interrupted, Sadie decided it was time for the children to get a little fresh air before lunch. She invited Maria to eat with them but Maria declined, saying she'd take her break in the workshop with the men when they came in to eat the meals they'd brought from home.

"Feel free to drop by again. It's nice to have a woman around here to talk to."

"I feel the same way," Sadie told her. But now that she had new insight about Levi, she didn't mind the prospect of chatting with him again, either.

"Something smells *appenditlich*," Levi commented after he said grace. It really did; he wasn't just trying to butter Sadie up and influence her decision to stay.

"It's stew." Sadie placed the pot on a trivet in the center of the table to serve them. Her cheeks were flushed and the children's faces were ruddy, too.

"Did you go outside this morning?"

"*Jah*, but we didn't go any farther than the barn. You said we could," Sadie quickly reminded him, as if she was afraid they'd get in trouble. Had he really come across as that prohibitive this morning? No wonder she was considering whether to stay or not.

"Oh, *gut*. I was only asking because your complexion looks pretty…" he began but stopped midsentence to concentrate on not spilling the full bowl of stew Sadie handed him. When he set it down in front of him, he suddenly realized what he'd said and rushed to clarify. "I meant to say your skin looks pretty pink. *Very* pink, that is, not pretty. Although it's not *not* pretty, either. David's and Elizabeth's faces are extremely pink, as well."

Levi was certain his face was the pinkest of them all as Sadie bit back a smile and graciously switched subjects. "We stopped in the workshop and said hello to Maria, too."

"She let us make ornaments," David said.

"But the *kinner* didn't go anywhere near Maria's shears," Sadie informed him. "Or get too close to the woodstove."

Levi blinked. Was Sadie mocking him? Or was she trying to reassure him she took his concerns seriously? If so, Levi appreciated it, although he wondered what accounted for her sudden change in attitude.

"Then we played Freeze Tag in the yard. It's like tag but you have to freeze in place like this." David leaped up from his chair and struck a pose, causing Levi to chuckle. His laughter grew louder the longer David remained motionless, refusing to even blink.

"All right, sit down and eat your lunch now," he finally directed his son.

"You have to tag him first." Elizabeth walked around the table and tapped her brother on the shoulder. "Like that."

"*Denki*, Elizabeth. I was getting starved," David said appreciatively, taking his seat again.

Tickled by their cheerful behavior, Levi turned his attention to Sadie. It occurred to him he'd been so preoccupied with his own concerns that morning he hadn't asked Sadie to tell him anything about herself.

"I'd like to hear more about your life in Pennsylvania. Do you work as a nanny there, too?"

"*Neh*, I worked in a furniture store." She blew on a spoonful of meat. "But sales were in decline and the owner couldn't employ two clerks, so here I am."

Relieved by her response, Levi said, "We're glad you are, aren't we, *kinner*?" Their mouths were full, but they nodded vigorously.

He tried to think of something else to ask Sadie but

his mind went blank, so they ate in silence. Once their meal was over, Sadie suggested the children take picture books to their rooms and told them she'd be up to tuck them in for their naps after she finished the dishes.

When Elizabeth paused in the doorway and asked, "Will you still be here when we wake up, Sadie?" Levi felt a prick of guilt, remembering how their second nanny actually *did* leave when the children were napping. She was so peeved about something he'd said she didn't even finish out the day.

"Of course I will. I'm staying until the day before Grischtdaag."

Her answer elicited cheers from the children. Over their heads Levi caught Sadie's eye and mouthed, *Denki*.

When she nodded and smiled back it occurred to him his household was beginning to experience the return of joy. Maybe David was right; maybe Christmas was when wonderful things happened.

Chapter Three

On Tuesday morning it was Levi who answered the door because the children were still getting dressed. "They fell asleep right away last night, so I thought they'd be up bright and early today but I had a difficult time rousing them."

Suspecting they were tired because she'd run their legs off playing Freeze Tag yesterday, Sadie stifled a smile. There was no need to gloat. "My guess is they'll be hungrier than usual this morning, so I'll make *pannekuche* and *wascht* for breakfast." She'd taken inventory of the pantry the day before, so she knew Levi had the ingredients for pancakes on hand and there was sausage in the fridge.

"*Denki*. I already put on a pot of *kaffi*. Would you like me to pour you a cup before I go see to the milking?"

Pleased by the gesture, Sadie accepted. As she mixed the batter, she hummed softly. Clearly Levi intended this day to get off to a much better start and so did she. The children were their usual cheerful selves, although David couldn't stop yawning.

"Schlofkopp." Levi affectionately called his son a sleepyhead. "If you and your *schweschder* had gotten up earlier, we could have taken Sadie on a tour of the farm. Now it's too late. I have to go meet the crew."

"That's all right," Sadie assured him. "We'll run around in the yard or walk to the barn like we did yesterday."

Levi shot her a grateful look. "If we have a quick lunch this afternoon, I'll have time to show you around then. That way, you and the *kinner* will have more options for your outdoor activities."

"If you're sure you don't mind, we'd really like that," Sadie replied.

"It would be my pleasure."

Elizabeth screwed up her face and asked, "Why are you and Sadie talking funny, Daed? It sounds *narrish*."

"Elizabeth," Levi admonished, "that's not any way for a *kind* to speak to her *eldre*."

Elizabeth apologized, but Sadie silently admired how astute the child was; Sadie and Levi *were* being overly polite and their conversation sounded artificial to her ears, too. Although it was better than the previous day's tense discussions, Sadie hoped in time they'd relax around each other enough to talk naturally.

After Levi left, Sadie washed the dishes while the children brushed their teeth, made their beds and took turns sweeping the floors. Then she read to them from the Bible and helped them practice writing their names before they went outside, where Sadie taught them how to play Simon Says and Mother, May I, followed by another round of Freeze Tag.

She must have needed more time to get used to the climate because Sadie wanted to go back inside before the children did. "If we keep playing Freeze Tag, I'm going to freeze for real!"

"Five more minutes, please?" Elizabeth cajoled and David echoed her request.

Sadie realized playing outdoors was so new to them they probably felt like they couldn't get enough of it, so she gave in to their request. After another twenty minutes of chasing each other, they returned to the house to warm up and make hot chocolate, which they then brought to the workshop to share with Maria.

"You must have known I needed your help again, Elizabeth and David," Maria said. "Would you like to decorate one of the trunk ornaments you made yesterday? We'll hang them up as examples for the *Englisch kinner.*"

"Do you need my help, too?" Sadie asked as Maria situated the children at their workbench, out of earshot.

"I won't turn it down, that's for sure. We're shipping these to our vendors on Thursday and then I'll assemble more for sale here. I'm worried I won't have enough made by the time we open, especially since I won't be here next Tuesday." Maria snapped her fingers and set down her mug. "*Ach!* That reminds me, I have something for you."

"What's this?" Sadie asked instead of opening the envelope Maria had fished from her tote bag and handed to her.

"It's from Grace Bawell. You didn't get to meet her Sunday because she was visiting relatives in Unity but I saw her yesterday evening and she asked me to deliver this to you. It's a note inviting you to her *hochzich.* She wanted to invite you in person, but she's so busy with the preparations she can't make the trip over here."

"An invitation to her *hochzich*?" Sadie repeated blankly. She felt as if her face were made of brick and she couldn't have smiled if she wanted to.

"*Jah*, a week from today. I can't wait. I love *hochzichen!*"

"Well, I don't." The words escaped her lips before Sadie could stop them and she scrambled for something to say that wouldn't sound rude. She repeated, "Well, I don't...want her to feel like she has to invite me just because I arrived at the wrong time—at the last minute, I mean."

"That's *narrish*. Open it. Read her note. She really wants you there."

Sadie unsealed the envelope and scanned the card for details. On the bottom in tiny print, Grace had written, *I truly hope you'll come, Sadie! I can't wait to meet you and introduce you to my husband (to-be). Until then, may the Lord bless you—Grace.* Sadie's groan was audible.

"What's wrong? You're acting as if you've been summoned to a funeral, not invited to a *hochzich*."

Realizing how ill-mannered she appeared, Sadie said, "It's lovely of Grace to invite me, but...but Levi might not give me the day off."

"*Lappich!* Levi and the *kinner* will be attending, too. I don't know how your district does things in Pennsylvania, but here in Serenity Ridge, we close our businesses and the teacher and scholars take the day off school for *hochzichen*, too. The entire church is expected to go—it would be unthinkable for anyone to stay home."

Of course, that was exactly how things were done in Sadie's district, but she'd been hoping it was different in Maine. She stammered, "I, uh, I guess I'll be there, then."

Maria clapped. "*Gut!* And don't worry about being new here and not knowing anyone—Grace will pair you up with a friendly bachelor for supper."

"*Neh*, she shouldn't do that!" Sadie objected.

Amish weddings lasted all day. There was the three-hour church service and ceremony, which was followed by a big dinner. Guests socialized, sang and played games throughout the afternoon, and in the evening there was a second, informal meal. It was tradition for the bride and sometimes the groom to play matchmaker, seating young, unmarried people together for supper.

"Why not? Do you have a suitor back in Pennsylvania?"

"Back in Pennsylvania, I wouldn't tell you if I did," Sadie retorted, irritated by Maria's persistence. "We consider courting to be a private matter."

Maria blinked rapidly and the tips of her ears went red. "I didn't mean to intrude. I'm sorry."

Sadie felt terrible; her new friend was only trying to make her feel welcome. "You have no reason to apologize. I'm the one who's being rude and I'm sorry. It's just that I came to Maine to *avoid* going to *hochzichen*."

In a hushed tone she described what had happened—what *hadn't* happened—between her and Harrison. Abashed, Sadie concluded by telling Maria she'd decided to put all thoughts of romance out of her mind so she wouldn't be so desperate to be in a courtship that she made a mistake like that again.

"I understand why you wouldn't want to attend Harrison's *hochzich*, but I'm not sure you can just make up your mind you're finished with romance," Maria countered. "It has a way of creeping up on you."

Sadie giggled. "You make it sound like catching the flu. Which might actually be an accurate comparison, judging from my experience."

Waving a bough at her, Maria said, "That's because you haven't met the right man yet."

"I don't want to. Not right now and certainly not here, since I'm going home in a month." Sadie fiddled with a lopsided bow, pulling it straight before venturing to ask, "You said you love *hochzichen*, but be honest. Doesn't it bother you to watch *meed* much younger than you getting married?"

"Are you asking if I feel like a bitter old maid? I'm only thirty-one, you know. That's hardly ancient."

"*Neh*, I didn't mean it like that—"

"It's okay," Maria said with a laugh. "But *neh*, it doesn't bother me, because I wouldn't want to marry the men they're marrying. Not that they're not *wunderbaar* men, because they are. But their suitors wouldn't have been the man for *me*. I'd rather wait however long it takes to marry the man Gott intends for me to marry than get married simply because I've reached a certain age."

"Then you still think…" Sadie realized the question was rude, so she let her sentence dangle but Maria seemed to read her thought.

"Do I think there *is* a man out there the Lord has intended for me to marry?" Maria didn't hesitate to answer. "*Jah*, I do. And I think there's one out there for you, too. Like it or not!"

Sadie was about to say, "I won't hold my breath," but

Maria looked so earnest Sadie changed her mind and forced a laugh in spite of herself.

After lunch Levi pushed aside his plate, unfolded a small map and laid it flat it on the table. "The printer delivered these this morning, so I brought you one," he told Sadie, who pinched her lips together. Was she irritated or amused? "I had them made for the customers so they'd know how to navigate back to the exit once they've chosen their trees, but I thought you could use one, as well. Not that you'll get lost, but I wanted us to have a common reference point. This way, if I tell you what part of the farm I'm working on and later you need to find me, you can just look at this. All the sections and rows are labeled."

"That was a *gut* idea. *Denki*." Sadie smiled, relaxing at his explanation and coming around to his side of the table. As she leaned to examine the map, her sleeve brushed against his. She traced a marking with her slender finger. "What does this symbol indicate?"

"That's the pond." Acutely aware he hadn't been in such close proximity to a woman in ages, Levi was suddenly nervous. He didn't want to intrude on Sadie's personal space, so he sat as motionless as David had been when he demonstrated how to play Freeze Tag.

"Is this thing in the middle of the pond a duck?"

Levi chuckled. "That's a caution flag, so the customers know to keep their *kinner* from wandering off to the other side of the barn. The printer duplicated my original sketch. I guess I should have asked David or Elizabeth to help with the drawing."

Sadie giggled and stood straight again. Collecting the dirty plates from the table, she asked, "Now that I have the map, does that mean you're not giving me a personal tour?"

Is she relieved...or disappointed? Levi couldn't tell from the levity of her tone. Before he could say it was her choice, David spoke up.

"Aw, Daed, you promised we could show Sadie our farm and help you point out hazards she might not have in Pennsylvania."

"David!" Elizabeth admonished. "You were supposed to be secret about that so Sadie doesn't think Daed is too bossy."

Levi cringed, but Sadie calmly replied, "That's okay, Elizabeth, I won't think your *daed* is being too bossy. I'll think he just wants us to be safe."

"We can't be safe if we don't help point out the hazards," David reasoned.

Levi caught Sadie's eye and shrugged. "It's up to you."

"Then *jah*, let's take a tour of the hazards," Sadie replied with a wink that caused Levi to grin from ear to ear. "You three go put on your coats while I finish rinsing the dishes."

When Levi and the children had donned their outerwear and Sadie still didn't come to the mudroom, Levi brought her jacket to her in the kitchen. Holding it up so she could slip her arms into it, he asked, "Are you going to be cold? This coat seems kind of thin."

"I'll be fine. Tomboys are tough," she said as Elizabeth came into the room.

"Daed, you tied my scarf too tight. My neck is choking," she complained, so Sadie loosened it for her before they finally set out on their trek.

Sadie was so inquisitive about the farm and so appreciative of the beauty of the landscape it seemed time stood still as the foursome made their way around the property. Since Levi's break was already half-over, they didn't get to cover the entire farm, but he showed Sadie a sizable section of the acreage—including the "hazardous" pond, "treacherous" rocks and the "precarious" run-down shack on his neighbor's property—before she began to shiver. *I knew that coat wasn't warm enough for her. It's too bad I donated my* mamm's *clothing or I could have given Sadie her wool coat.*

"Does anyone want a mug of hot chocolate?" she asked when they returned. The children said yes, so she directed them into the living room to warm up by the woodstove while she heated the milk. "Would you like some, too, Levi?"

He'd already taken twice as long as he usually took for a lunch break, but the afternoon had been so pleasant he wanted to draw it out. "*Jah*, please. While you're making it, I'll bring in more wood. I can hear your teeth chattering from here. I'll get the fire roaring and then we can drink our cocoa in the living room."

When he returned, there were two mugs and two plates holding thin slices of shoofly pie on the kitchen table. Sadie raised a finger to her lips and pointed to the living room with her other hand. "The twins couldn't hold out until nap time. I'll stoke the fire later. I don't want to wake them—I brought the leftover pie from church and there's really enough for two people. I was going to give it to the *kinner*, but..."

"Their loss is our gain," Levi jested. When he pulled his chair away from the table, it loudly scraped against the floor. He and Sadie simultaneously stopped moving and cocked their ears toward the living room, but they didn't hear the children stirring, so they took their seats.

With his fork suspended above the plate, Levi whispered, "I feel like we're doing something we shouldn't be doing."

"*Jah*, this reminds me of when my *brieder* and I used to sneak cookies from the cookie jar when my mother's back was turned."

"I hope the *kinner* don't catch us—we'll get sent to our rooms without any dinner."

"I could be the lookout while you eat your piece and then we can trade places," Sadie joked and her muted laugh tickled her throat, which made her face go red and her eyes water.

"You okay?" Levi asked nervously. "Are you choking? Do you need water?"

"I'm fine," she croaked, waving her hand. It took another moment for her to catch her breath, and when she did, she said, "Oh, *neh*. Look, my sleeve is all wet. I must have spilled hot chocolate. I hope my manners are better at Grace's *hochzich*."

"Ah, the *hochzich*. I forgot about that," Levi flatly remarked. *I tried to forget about it anyway.* Ever since Leora died, weddings depressed him.

"You're going, aren't you? Because I'd like to ride with you if I may."

"*Jah*. Unless there's a blizzard," Levi said. Without thinking, he muttered, "Sadly, there's little hope of that."

Sadie lifted her eyebrows. "You don't want to go, either?"

"Either? Does that mean *you* don't want to go? Why not?" He asked his questions in rapid succession.

"You tell me why you don't want to go first."

Levi stalled. He couldn't express the real reason to

Sadie, that weddings reminded him of all the hopes he and Leora once had for their life together. They reminded him of losing her. Of how she died. Of what he'd never have again, what he didn't deserve to have: a wife. "Oh, er, it's that they last all day and it's hard on the *kinner* to miss their naps. They get cranky and then I worry they'll misbehave," he said and he meant it, too, even if that wasn't the primary reason. "Why don't you want to go?"

"I—I won't really know anyone there. I haven't even met the bride or groom yet."

Was that really the reason? Sadie didn't seem particularly shy. Regardless, etiquette required them both to be there, so Levi replied, "Then we should stick together. That way, you can help with the *kinner* and I'll introduce you to everyone. How does that sound?"

"Not quite as *gut* as a blizzard, but I like it," Sadie said and Levi didn't know if it was her smile or the hot chocolate warming his insides like that.

Sadie whistled as she slid a blueberry pie from the oven and placed it on a tray. Viscous, deep purple liquid bubbled within the golden-brown lattice piecrust. It was customary for guests to bring food to Amish weddings, and when Sadie mentioned she didn't know what to make, Levi had recalled he and the children had picked so many blueberries that summer he'd ended up freezing the surplus. When Sadie asked if that was a hint, he'd admitted blueberry pie was his favorite and told her that once she tasted Maine blueberries it would be her favorite, too. And he was right; the blueberries were especially plump and sweet. Content her pie appeared to have turned out beautifully, Sadie busied herself wrapping her gift—the two sets of bath and hand towels she'd bought when Levi took her to the nearest department store on Saturday evening. She'd helped Maria make so many bows her fingers flew into action and within a minute she topped the box with a large silver bow. After that, all she had left to do was straighten her prayer *kapp* and put on her coat.

She positioned the rocking chair in front of the window so she could catch sight of the buggy starting down the driveway. While she was waiting, she reflected on how smoothly the week had gone. She had established a balanced routine for the children. After breakfast and chores, she usually read them a Bible story. Then they'd examine the map and choose where they wanted to play or explore for the rest of the morning. Levi came home at lunchtime and afterward the children napped while Sadie took care of the dishes and spent quiet time in prayer or reading Scripture. When the twins woke, they'd all head outside to play again, and following that, they'd help Maria in the workshop until it was time for Sadie to prepare supper.

Maria said their visits were the best part of her day and insisted she wanted them all to spend Thanksgiving at her house, too. At first Sadie hesitated, knowing Maria lived alone with her mother, who was recovering from a broken hip, and that Maria's aunt was visiting to help. The women probably had enough work on their hands. But Maria insisted the children's presence would cheer her mother, and when Elizabeth and David overheard the conversation they pleaded with Sadie until she agreed to consult Levi about it.

To her surprise, he enthusiastically accepted the invitation, saying, "Otherwise, we'll end up having buttered noodles for dinner. That's one of the few things I know how to make."

"*I* could make Thanksgiving dinner," Sadie suggested before it occurred to her she was being presumptuous; perhaps Levi didn't want to spend Thanksgiving with her.

"*Neh*. You cook for us every day. You deserve a day off and I think Maria truly wants to host us. Years ago she told Leora how quiet her house was at the holidays ever since her *daed* died and her *bruder* got married. He goes to his in-laws' house in Unity for Thanksgiving and that's too far of a trip for Maria's mother to make while her hip is mending."

As she rocked back and forth, Sadie reflected on how sensitive Levi was to Maria's needs, as well as to her own. She was glad she could reciprocate by helping him mind the children at the wedding—and doubly glad because she figured taking care of David and Elizabeth would keep her mind off the fact that last year at this time, she'd prayed she'd be hosting her own wedding instead of attending someone else's during this year's wedding season.

A knock startled Sadie to her feet. She hadn't seen or heard the buggy in the driveway yet and when she opened the door, she found out why: Elizabeth stood there, red-faced and sniffling, her hair hanging down to her shoulders and her face wet with tears. Levi stood behind her, one hand resting on her shoulder, the other holding a hairbrush, and David was behind him, hopping from one foot to the other.

Recognizing the problem at once, Sadie exclaimed, "Oh, *gut*, I was hoping you'd let me fix your hair instead of letting your *daed* do it for you today, Elizabeth. A *hochzich* is a special occasion and a *maedel* wants to look her best, even if she's not the one getting married, right?"

Elizabeth wiped her palm across her pudgy cheek and gave a forlorn nod, so Sadie told her to go have a seat in the rocking chair.

"Sorry about this. She usually doesn't mind that I can't do her hair as neat as some of the other *meed*'s," Levi whispered. "But today she—wow, that *blohbier* pie smells *appenditlich*."

Sadie laughed at how easily distracted he was by the dessert. "I'd ask you to carry it to the buggy for me, but I don't think I trust you with it."

"That's probably a smart move. How about if I carry this instead?" Levi picked up the gift and said he and David would have the buggy ready and waiting.

When Sadie and Elizabeth approached a few moments later, Levi jumped down to assist them into the carriage. "Your hair looks very pretty," he told his daughter, even though her church bonnet was covering her head.

"Sadie braided it just like hers."

"Hers looks pretty, too," he replied, and even though Sadie knew he was forced to say it, she felt a flush of shyness.

"You both look your best and you're going to act your best, too, right, *kinner*?" Levi prompted his children.

As it turned out, the reminder was unnecessary; David and Elizabeth didn't so much as fidget throughout the long wedding service. The same couldn't be said for Sadie. As much as she tried not to think about how much she wished *she* were the one taking her wedding vows, the longing gnawed at her like a hunger pang and she squirmed in her seat.

When the service ended, she was torn between helping the women prepare the food and supervising the twins and the other children in the designated playroom in the basement of the church. But Levi helped make the decision for her.

"Would you mind keeping an eye on David and Elizabeth while I help set up tables?" During Amish weddings in Serenity Ridge, as in Little Springs, after the service the men arranged tables and chairs around the periphery of the gathering room and the guests sat facing the center so they could see each other as they partook of the wedding meal.

Within an hour, Levi returned to where Sadie was encouraging two six-year-old girls to share a box of blocks with their brother while David and Elizabeth quietly pieced together a puzzle in the corner. Levi told Sadie dinner was being served and since the district was so small, they wouldn't have to take turns to eat, the way guests usually did at the large Amish weddings in Little Springs. But he said the seats were filling fast. "If we scuttle upstairs before the rest of the *eldre* and *kinner* do, we can sit together as a *familye*, otherwise we might get split up."

Sadie dropped her head to hide her blush, but Levi was so focused on signaling the twins to follow him upstairs he didn't seem to realize he'd referred to Sadie as family. And in fact, eating together felt familiar, if not familial, since the foursome dined together every day at Levi's house. By the time dessert was served, it was no longer an effort for Sadie to keep from dwelling on her status as a single woman or to push thoughts of courtship and marriage from her mind. Those disappointments were replaced by a sense of belonging, and she enjoyed the festivities more than she expected she would. It helped that several people stopped by their table to compliment Sadie on the blueberry pie she'd made.

"If you'll excuse me for not waiting until the *kinner* are done eating, I'd better go get a piece," Levi said. But he returned from the dessert table empty-handed, yammering, "I was too late. It was all gone."

"All the dessert is gone?" Elizabeth fussed. She was finishing her second helping of filling—also known as stuffing—mixed with chicken, a wedding meal staple.

"*Neh*, just all of Sadie's pie," he replied. "There are plenty of other goodies, but my mouth was watering for a taste of that *blohbier* pie."

"Maybe Sadie will make another one just for us," David suggested, licking gravy from his spoon.

"*Jah*, we'll pick more *blohbieren*," Elizabeth volunteered.

"It's not *blohbier* season until summer," Levi reminded them. "Sadie is only here until Grischtdaag."

Whispering audibly, David advised, "If you're really nice and say please she might stay until *blohbier* season, Daed."

"I'll keep that in mind, *suh*," Levi whispered back, also loudly enough for Sadie to hear. Although she knew he was only placating his child, Levi's response tickled her heart. And just like that, she was thinking about romance again.

Levi didn't anticipate staying at the wedding until the second meal, but it had been so long since he'd spent any time socializing that nearly everyone wanted to chat with him. He was glad to catch up on their lives, too. Recalling Sadie said she felt self-conscious as a newcomer, he made a point to introduce her to additional church members. Some of them tried to persuade her to join the young adults playing board games, but she declined. Figuring she felt obligated to help keep tabs on David and Elizabeth, Levi realized he ought to insist he could watch the children himself, but he didn't. There was something about having Sadie at his side that kept at bay the dejection he usually experienced during weddings. Whether it was the zip in her eyes or the pertness of her smile, her cheerfulness was contagious and he reveled in it.

He'd hardly had time to get hungry again before the smell of supper drifted downstairs to where he was standing with Sadie in the far corner of the playroom, chatting as they kept their eyes on the twins and the other children whose parents were upstairs.

"There you are!" the bride called as she approached them with Maria at her side. "I've been looking for you, Sadie. There's someone I want to seat you with at supper."

Levi was well aware of this matchmaking custom, but he'd taken it for granted Sadie would eat with his family again, even though he'd noticed a couple of Grace's bachelor cousins trying to catch Sadie's eye. Although Sadie had never specifically said she didn't have a suitor, Levi figured if she was being courted she wouldn't have left Pennsylvania, nor would Grace have been trying to pair her up—women had a way of knowing these things about each other.

"*Denki*, but I—I think Levi needs my help with the

kinner, don't you, Levi?" She nudged him with her elbow and looked sideways at him.

What did her expression mean? Was she asking his permission to eat with the others? That was ridiculous. He had the day off work; she should have it off, too. It occurred to him he was being selfish. He wanted to say that of course she should go eat with the others, but the words stuck in his throat.

"I'll sit at Levi's table and help him with the *kinner*," Maria volunteered.

Aware he would offend both Sadie and Maria by indicating he'd hoped Sadie would eat with him, Levi did his best to sound convincing as he replied, "*Denki*, Maria. I'd really like your company. Sadie, you absolutely ought to go meet the young man Grace has paired you with."

Maria beamed. "I'll round up the twins. Have *schpass*, Sadie."

"I think you and Jonathan will really hit it off. He's from Pennsylvania, too," Levi overheard Grace gushing as she took Sadie by the arm and led her across the room.

They were almost out the door when Sadie stopped and called over her shoulder, "There's no need for you to wait for me when you're ready to go, Levi. Grace says she's certain one of the young people will give me a ride back to the farm."

Then, before he could say goodbye, she was gone and so was the serenity Levi had experienced throughout the day. In its place was a familiar and pervasive gloominess he couldn't shake for the rest of the evening, no matter how hard he tried.

Chapter Four

I am such a dummkopf! Sadie wrote in her diary after Grace's great-aunt and uncle gave her a ride home from the wedding early Tuesday evening. *Once again, I actually thought a man—this time, Levi—was showing signs he was romantically interested in me, only to find out he's interested in someone else. How could I have been so wrong again?*

I knew when he made the remark about my hair looking nice that he had to say it because Elizabeth's was done the same way. And I was aware he only told David he'd consider asking me to stay in Maine longer to appease his son. I could even dismiss his slipup in referring to the four of us as a family. But I truly thought he felt something more for me from the way he acted during lunch and throughout the afternoon—hanging on to my every word and laughing at every joke I made, no matter how silly. It's true he could have just enjoyed joking around with me, as a friend, but when other people came to chat with him, I'd catch him gazing my way, as if he couldn't take his eyes off me. And then he followed me downstairs to mind everyone's children—men never do that kind of thing at church gatherings. I suppose it's possible Levi didn't think I'd keep a close enough watch on Elizabeth and David in a new setting, but when we got to the basement, I don't think he glanced at Elizabeth and David more than once or twice. It was as if he only came downstairs to talk to me.

But I must have been vain or kidding myself to think he was paying special attention to me, because he sure jumped at the chance to have supper with Maria. If he had even a smidgen of romantic interest in me he wouldn't have insisted I go eat with another man.

As if that wasn't upsetting enough, Jonathan was the smuggest person I've ever met! I hadn't sat down with him for more than three minutes when he said, "I should make something clear. I'm walking out with someone back home. Grace doesn't know about her, so that's probably why she paired me with you. I wouldn't want you to think I asked for this introduction."

I wanted to tell him not to flatter himself, but I couldn't be that rude, even if he deserved it. So I said, "That's okay, I'm only humoring Grace, too. Since it's tradition for brides to play matchmaker at their weddings, I think it's important for single guests to politely accept being paired together, whether or not they have anything in common, don't you?"

You would have thought he'd catch on, but instead he acted as if it came as a huge relief I wasn't interested in him. He said, "Gut, I'm glad to hear that. I've been to a lot of weddings and I've been paired with a lot of meed. *You wouldn't believe how many of them get their noses bent out of shape when I don't end the meal by asking to court them. They assume the bride seated us together because I had an interest in them—even if I wasn't showing any interest at all. I mean, I've tried to act like a gentleman and engage in friendly conversation, but a lot of* meed *still get the wrong idea. So now I tell them right off the bat I'm already courting. It saves us both a lot of trouble."*

After listening to Jonathan talk like that, I realized Levi was probably just being polite and friendly to me earlier because that's how gentlemen should behave at weddings. I was interpreting it wrong because it's such a festive, love-focused occasion I got carried away with romantic ideas. If Levi knew the direction my thoughts had taken, he'd probably feel the same way about me that Jonathan felt about those other women. So I guess if there's any consolation, it's that I didn't let on about my feelings. Tomorrow I'll go about my business as if nothing's different. Which it isn't, because I'm not interested in romance; I was just temporarily influenced by the wedding atmosphere, that's all.

But that doesn't mean I'm not upset with Maria. She knew *how I felt about not wanting to be paired with anyone, yet she practically led Grace to me by the hand. Why would she do that when I specifically told her not to? My guess is she wanted to be alone with Levi. After all, didn't she say she used to be close to Leora and she still likes Levi a lot? Judging from his enthusiasm about sitting with her, Levi is probably drawn to Maria, too. Which is of no concern to me. But then Maria should have been honest about it instead of allowing Grace to match me up with Jonathan. I would have preferred taking Elizabeth and David to the children's table and eating supper with them there than to have to listen to Jonathan!*

It's no wonder Maria doesn't feel anxious about

being over thirty and being unmarried still—she's got
her sights set on Levi. That's probably why she said
she'd hate for Levi to lose me, too; she wants him to
have a nanny so they can walk out in the evenings. For
all I know, he's the reason she invited us to celebrate
Thanksgiving at her house—and it's probably why he
was so willing to accept the invitation. That's fine if
they want to court, but I refuse to be the third wheel on
Thursday. Thanksgiving is a holiday, so I shouldn't be
expected to mind the children just so Levi and Maria
can be together. I'm going to tell them both tomorrow
to count me out!

Sadie slapped her diary shut and set it on the nightstand. Staring at the ceiling, she reflected on how unfair
she thought it was that although Grace was only twenty
and Maria was thirty-one and they lived in a tiny settlement in the middle of nowhere, they had both managed
to find suitors. Yet Sadie lived in one of the counties
with the highest Amish population in the country and
she had no prospects. None. *Why not, Lord? Why not?*
she prayed, catching a tear before it rolled down her
cheek and into her ear.

But knowing *why* she didn't have a suitor when
someone else did wasn't going to make her feel any
better about not having one. No, the only way to feel
better was to accept her circumstances and learn to be
content with them. That was why she'd come to Maine
after all. *I had no idea it was going to be this hard,*
though, she thought before removing her prayer *kapp*
and rolling over so she could sleep.

Levi lay in bed straining his ears to hear a buggy approaching. It was almost midnight already and as far as

he knew Sadie still wasn't home. Of course, she might have arrived when he was giving the children baths—they were both wound up from eating too much sugar and he'd thought the warm water would settle them down—but probably not. Sadie clearly didn't have any intention of coming home early; otherwise she would have ridden with him.

He couldn't fault her for that. She was young; young people were interested in courting, or at least in spending time with other young people of the opposite gender. Even though they'd agreed to stick together at the wedding, Levi wondered if she felt resentful she had to stay with him and the children. If she did, he never would have guessed it from her mood throughout the day. She'd practically sparkled; she was so elated anyone might have thought *she* was the one getting married.

An image of Leora on their wedding day flashed through his mind, instantaneously followed—as always—by an image of her plain wooden casket being lowered into the ground. Levi shuddered. Thanks to Sadie distracting him with her warmth and witticisms, he'd gotten through the better part of the day without recalling Leora's funeral. Without wishing he was getting married all over again. Or wishing he'd been a better husband.

I had my opportunity, he thought. *I should have been more careful. I should have been more considerate of my precious wife.* He closed his eyes tightly, as if to squeeze the memory from his mind. It didn't work. It never did.

The knot in his neck rivaled the one in his throat. Sleepless, he counted as the clock chimed twelve times. Since he hadn't heard a buggy coming up the lane, he concluded Sadie must still be out. *I hope keeping a late*

*evening doesn't interfere with her ability to provide care
for the* kinner *tomorrow. I imagine she'll be exhausted.*

Indeed, the next morning Sadie appeared as fatigued
as *he* felt. "You look like you could use a cup of *kaffi*,"
he said after she'd come into the house and hung her
coat on the peg in the mudroom. "You must have been
out late last night socializing."

Instead of giving him the information he was admittedly curious about, she retorted with an edge in her
voice, "*You* look as if you could use a cup, yourself."

Ach. He knew better than to mention when a woman
looked tired; it wasn't meant to be an insult, but it was
usually taken as one. So he laughed and said, "*Jah*, I
had a late night. So did Elizabeth and David. Between
the wedding celebration and the wedding food, their
senses were overstimulated. I gave them baths and read
to them. I even told them made-up stories that were so
boring they nearly put *me* to sleep, but they chatted
away until almost ten. I hope they're not like this after
Thanksgiving, too."

Sadie set down her mug. "I'm glad you brought that
up, because I've decided I'd prefer not to go to Maria's
haus for Thanksgiving with you and the *kinner*. I mean,
it's not as if *you'll* be working, so I don't feel I should
be required to watch the twins. Besides, Maria will be
happy to help you watch them."

*She must have been invited to share Thanksgiving
dinner with Jonathan's* familye *at the Bawell* haus.
Levi wasn't surprised she'd want to see him again, but
Sadie had already accepted the invitation to Maria's
and he thought it was inconsiderate of her to change her
mind at the last minute. And if he were honest, he had
to admit the prospect of spending the afternoon with

Maria and her mother and aunt didn't seem as much fun without Sadie.

"Changing your mind like that doesn't seem like a very fair or thoughtful thing to do," he said, not bothering to conceal his disappointment.

"Well, I don't think it's fair to expect me to work on a holiday."

So, he was right; she did resent spending extra time with him and the children. How foolish he'd been to think she'd actually want to be with them when she wasn't being paid to be. Levi couldn't demand she honor her commitment to spend Thanksgiving with them, but he didn't want to make her decision any easier on her, either. "I think Maria will be disappointed you aren't coming."

"That's unlikely, but I'll work that out with her myself. Since I already told Maria I'd bring dessert and she probably won't have time to whip anything up at short notice, I'll make a couple of pies this afternoon for you to take with you."

"Are we having pie?" Elizabeth asked from the doorway, rubbing her eyes.

"Not today, you're not," Levi replied, cupping his daughter's chin in his hand and tilting her face upward. It occurred to him the children would be as disappointed as he was that Sadie wasn't coming to dinner at Maria's house, and suddenly he was doubly annoyed. Not only would he miss having Sadie there, but she was going to upset the children, too.

To Elizabeth he said, "You can have a piece of the pie Sadie sends with us to Maria's *haus* for Thanksgiving tomorrow."

"Isn't Sadie coming with us, Daed?" Elizabeth questioned. "You said she was."

Levi glanced in Sadie's direction; her back was turned and she was fiddling with something in the sink. "*Neh.* Thanksgiving is a holiday and Sadie doesn't have to be with us on holidays."

"But it won't be any *schpass* without her," Elizabeth sniveled. "I want her to be with us on the holidays."

I did, too, Levi thought.

I wish he hadn't told Elizabeth about my decision. Now she'll be pouty all morning. But unlike her daed, *at least* she *doesn't consider spending time with Maria to be as much* schpass *as spending time with me*, Sadie thought. Trying to mollify her, she said to Elizabeth, "Would you like to help me prepare the dough for the pies? Your *daed* doesn't allow you near the oven but I'll show you how to use the rolling pin."

Levi opened his mouth—was he going to say the rolling pin was dangerous, too?—but then closed it again and left the room to check on David. After he bade the children goodbye, he told Sadie not to make lunch for him. He said it was because he was still full from the wedding feast and he'd be too busy preparing the farm for the arrival of customers to take a break. Sadie doubted his excuses were true. Obviously he was irked she was ruining his Thanksgiving plans, but she didn't care; his romance with Maria wasn't her problem.

"Can we make pie now?" Elizabeth interrupted her thoughts.

"After you and David eat your breakfast. Meanwhile, I'll get the ingredients ready. What kind of pie should we make—apple or pumpkin?" Sadie actually planned to make both types of pie. She anticipated the children might each choose the opposite of what the other child wanted, so she'd brought spices she'd found in their grandmother's pantry to combine with ingredients Levi had in his.

"Pumpkin!" David declared.

"*Neh*, apple. Daed doesn't like pumpkin pie, 'member? Groossmammi never maked pumpkin pie because Daed doesn't like nutmeg and Groossmammi said a pumpkin pie without nutmeg isn't worth the energy it takes to make it," his sister reminded him.

Although it was sweet of Elizabeth to be so considerate of her father, Sadie's annoyance at him got the better of her. *I don't care if Elizabeth, Levi's mother and Maria all cater to his preferences. That doesn't mean I'm going to.*

"Which kind of pie do *you* like better, Elizabeth?" Sadie coaxed the answer from her.

"Pumpkin. With caramel and pecans on top."

"I don't like that stuff on mine," David objected.

His sister reprimanded him, "You can scrape it off if you don't like it but you shouldn't *say* you don't like it. That's not polite."

"Actually, I'm going to make *two* pumpkin pies," Sadie decided. "One with pecans and caramel and one without."

"What will Daed eat for dessert?"

Although she felt ever so slightly guilty, Sadie shrugged. "I guess Maria will have to make something sweet for him."

Her answer satisfied Elizabeth, who brought her dishes to the sink and climbed onto the stool to wash her hands. David didn't want to be left out, so he washed his hands, too. By the time the three of them finished rolling the crusts and preparing the filling, there was so much flour on the table it looked as if there had been a snow squall. One of Elizabeth's prayer *kapp* ribbons was sticky with caramel, and Sadie was almost positive David put some of the pecans he dropped on the floor back into the canister. But when Elizabeth announced if she was ever a nanny she was going to make a pie with the children because it was so much fun, Sadie knew the mess was worth it.

After Sadie slid the pies into the oven, David declared, "It's too bad Daed doesn't like nutmeg, because these are going to be the best pumpkin pies ever."

"He doesn't know what he's missing," Elizabeth said woefully and Sadie had to bite her lip so the children wouldn't see her smirking.

Levi pounded a sign into the nearly frozen earth, hoping the wood post wouldn't snap in two. His crew was palletizing the last of the tree shipments as he prepared the grounds for the arrival of customers. The other men had already helped him position long logs into place to indicate a parking lot perimeter on the same side of the yard as the barn. If more customers than expected showed up, they'd roll the logs back to expand the area, but Levi would cross that bridge if he came to it. Right now, he was positioning signs to indicate where customers could pick up handsaws, where they could locate the variety of tree they wanted— balsam, Fraser or Scotch—and of course, where they could pay for their purchases.

When he finished, Levi turned a slow circle, surveying the yard and farm. His Christmas tree lot was devoid of the strung lights and piped-in music many of the *Englisch* farms used to create a festive atmosphere, but the Amish didn't allow such material trappings. Furthermore, Levi didn't think they were necessary. If customers inhaled the pine-and-balsam scent of the trees, beheld the vibrant green of the conifers and slowed down enough to appreciate the relative quietude of the farm, they'd realize the beauty of God's creation was more than enough to make the season joyous.

Of course, Levi also hoped they'd find the perfect trees to take home for their celebrations. While not as grueling and unpredictable as other kinds of farming, growing full, healthy trees was more difficult than he and Leora had imagined. They'd quickly discovered the farm required nearly year-round care, including fertilizing, managing weeds and insects, and, of course, pruning. Now harvest time was finally here. *But Leora isn't*, Levi thought. It had been almost three years, and while grief no longer had a chokehold on him, during moments like this it was all Levi could do not to weep. He wished his wife was there to see their work and patience pay off.

"Everything looks *wunderbaar*," Maria said. Levi was so absorbed in his thoughts he hadn't seen her approach. "Only two more days! Leora would have been so pleased."

"You think so?" Levi felt the same way, but he was reassured by Maria's sentiment.

"*Jah*, although she would have said that sign is crooked," Maria replied and Levi laughed. Leora did have a way of fussing over small details, a point of contention between them during their marriage that seemed utterly insignificant now.

Straightening the signpost, Levi asked, "How are the wreaths coming along?"

The crew members had been transporting the wreaths from the racks in the workshop to bigger storage racks in the barn, but Levi trusted Maria implicitly, so he hadn't kept track of her progress.

"I'm getting there," she said quietly. Although raw gusts of air slapped at their faces, Levi noticed Maria's skin was more grayish than pink.

"Are you feeling okay?"

"I will be when we get back inside. *Kumme* see if you like where I set up the cash register counter," Maria said, motioning him toward the workshop.

The cash register was nothing more than a money box, and the counter was a high table near the door. Serenity Ridge's Amish business owners didn't accept credit cards; they only dealt in cash or checks. Levi realized this restriction might result in a loss of some sales, but when he spied the "ornaments" Elizabeth and David had made hanging above the crate of trunk slices, his worries vanished. One of his children had written *Joy*, on their ornament, and the other had written *Peace*. Their lopsided penmanship reminded him of how much they were looking forward to Christmas and of the real reason for celebrating.

Pointing, Levi said, "You must have helped them with those."

"*Neh*, Sadie did. They're fascinated by everything she says and does."

Levi had noticed the same thing, but he stopped short of agreeing aloud. Was Maria steadying herself against the workbench? "Are you sure you feel okay?"

"I'm fine but I need to get back to work if I'm going

to meet today's quota," Maria replied, picking up her hand shears and clipping a bough down to size.

"There is no *quota*, just an estimation of how many wreaths we'll need. I'd rather we have fewer sales than have you getting sick."

"Don't worry. I even plan to finish up here early this afternoon so I can skedaddle home and start Thanksgiving preparations. I noticed how much the *kinner* ate at the *hochzich*. Probably because Sadie has been running them ragged outside."

Now that Maria brought up the subject of Thanksgiving, Levi vacillated as to whether he should tell her of Sadie's change in plans. Neh, *that's Sadie's responsibility, not mine*, he ultimately decided. *And there's always a chance she might change her mind again.*

After the twins woke from their naps they took a jaunt with Sadie to the workshop, but at the door she told them she needed to speak to Maria alone. She instructed them to play in the side yard, where she could watch them from the window on the door.

Maria smiled wanly, as if she already knew what Sadie was about to say. "Hi, Sadie. I had to put away the *kinner*'s little workbench so it won't be in the way when the customers arrive, but now that you're here, I can pull it back out for them."

"The twins aren't coming in today. I wanted a moment to talk to you alone."

As Maria wiped her forehead with the back of her hand, Sadie noticed how peaked she looked. She was probably worn-out from socializing with Levi and getting ready to host him for Thanksgiving. "Oh, *gut*. I've been curious about last night. How did you and Jonathan get along?"

Sadie snapped, "We didn't! Other than the fact we both *kumme* from Pennsylvania, I have absolutely nothing in common with him."

"Oh, that's too bad." Maria frowned.

"*Neh*, what's too bad is how thoughtless you were to force me to sit with him just so you could get what you wanted. You knew I wasn't interested in courting. After how honest and vulnerable I've been, I expected a little more candor from you. If you had just told me, we could have worked something else out."

"I was being thoughtless to get what I wanted? What are you talking about?" Maria set down the hand shears and gripped the edge of the workbench. "I offered to take care of the *kinner* so you could meet a young man and maybe have a little *schpass* instead of babysitting all night. I was making a sacrifice."

"Ha! We both know it wasn't about me. You volunteered to take care of the *kinner* because you wanted to be with Levi and you know it," Sadie accused. "You like him a lot—you said as much."

"He was the husband of one of my closest friends! *Jah*, I like him, but not in a romantic way. The very thought of him as my suitor makes me—"

Maria abruptly covered her hand with her mouth and pushed past Sadie toward the door. She didn't have time to shut it behind her before she began retching. Sadie grabbed the damp cloth Maria used to wipe sap from her hands and rushed to her side. Elizabeth and David spotted them there and started trotting in their direction, but Sadie shook her finger, signaling them not to approach. Maria accepted the cloth from Sadie and blotted her lips with it.

"I didn't mean to imply Levi makes me retch," she joked weakly and tried to laugh, but then she was sick again.

Sadie stroked her friend's back, feeling terrible. She should have noticed the woman was genuinely ill, but she'd been so upset that she'd only seen what she wanted to see. When Maria stood upright again, Sadie extended her arm and led her to a chair inside the workshop. "You sit here and I'll go hitch your buggy to take you home."

Maria tried to stand but plunked right down in the chair again. "*Neh*, I'm okay. I can't leave. I haven't made nearly enough wreaths yet. Levi is counting on me. Besides, I gave Walker a ride today. I can't leave without him."

"You're sick and you need to go home and get to bed. I'll finish the wreaths if I have to work all night and all day tomorrow and tomorrow night, too. It's the least I can do," Sadie said penitently. "I'm so sorry, Maria. I was being overly sensitive."

"*Neh*, you have a right to be upset. You told me you weren't interested in romance, so I should have discouraged Grace from pairing you up. But I figured you do so much for Levi's *familye* that you deserved a break," Maria explained.

Sadie gave Maria a sideways embrace. "Please, let's put this behind us, okay?"

"Okay, but you have to believe me when I say I think of Levi like a *bruder*. A very sullen *bruder*. He hardly said two words the rest of the evening after you left. I think he would have preferred to eat with you, not me,"

Maria maintained. "Tell me, was it really that bad eating with Jonathan, too?"

"Let's put it this way…within thirty seconds he told me he was courting someone in Pennsylvania and he didn't want me to get my hopes up about him the way so many other *meed* did."

"He said that?"

"*Jah*, and he also belched six or seven times during the course of supper and not once did he excuse himself." When Maria groaned, Sadie said, "Oops, sorry for mentioning that. Are you still nauseated?"

Maria nodded. "If this keeps up, I don't know how I'll ever manage to make Thanksgiving dinner. I can hardly say the word, much less cook the food. I'm sorry—I was looking forward to all of you coming, and now it's too late for you to make other plans."

"Don't even think about that. I'll take care of dinner for Levi and the twins. Do you want me to make something to bring over to your *mamm*?"

"*Denki*, but she actually was sick last night, too, so I doubt she'll feel *gut* enough to eat anytime soon. Besides, my *ant* is there."

Just then the twins and Scott and Walker barged through the door, laughing loudly.

"Walker and Scott came to take the wreaths to the barn. They said we could help," David proudly reported.

"*Jah*. We finished everything we need to do before we open on Friday, so Levi said we could leave early this afternoon. He had to run to town to get cash for the cash box. Are you almost ready to go, Maria?"

Maria looked at Sadie. "If you're sure you can—"

Sadie didn't hesitate. "We'll finish up here without

any problem at all. I've watched you make so many wreaths I could do it in my sleep."

It wasn't until after Walker, Scott and Maria left and Elizabeth commented she was getting hungry that Sadie realized the only groceries Levi had purchased for Thanksgiving were the ingredients for dessert. Pumpkin pie, with nutmeg. *Levi's favorite*, she thought wryly. But what could she do about it now?

Levi pulled off his coat and hung it in the mudroom. The house was dim and quiet and he didn't smell anything cooking. His imagination scudded from one horrible scenario to another, the way it always did when the children weren't where he expected them to be. Without bothering to remove his boots, he strode to the living room and then called Elizabeth's and David's names as he charged up the stairs even though the hall and rooms were dark. *Breathe*, he told himself as he clomped back downstairs and outside onto the porch.

"Elizabeth! David! Sadie!" he called into the dark. No response. He started for the barn and on the way he noticed light coming from his workshop. Maria probably knew where they were. He sprinted to the little building, but before he even reached the door he could hear the children singing Christmas carols. Levi slowed his pace and released a sigh. Denki, *Lord*.

When he opened the door he immediately spotted Sadie at the clamping machine and Elizabeth gluing cord to a trunk slice. For some reason David was sitting on the floor atop a mound of scrappy boughs and pine needles.

"Hi, Daed. I'm an eagle. See my nest?" his son asked proudly.

"He's supposed to be helping make ornaments," Elizabeth tattled.

"Sadie said if I swept the floor I could use the branches to make a nest."

Levi held in a laugh and greeted Sadie, who explained Maria was ill and Walker had taken her home in her buggy. Because she hadn't made quite enough wreaths before she left, Sadie and the children had taken over for her, with Sadie assembling the boughs and the children making ornaments and cleaning the workshop. "I guess we lost track of time but we know how important opening day is, so we wanted to help. I'll go start supper now—I can *kumme* back later to finish putting ribbons on these and to tidy up the last of my mess."

Overwhelmed by Sadie's efforts to help him with both the twins and his business, Levi thanked her profusely. "After all the hard work the three of you did, you shouldn't have to make supper tonight. How about I take the *kinner* with me to the phone shanty and I'll order a pizza delivered?"

"*Jah*, pizza!" David exclaimed.

"Eagles don't eat pizza," Elizabeth informed him.

Sadie must have sensed an argument was about to erupt, because she set down the shears definitively and announced, "*Everyone* loves pizza, even eagles. While you're going to the shanty, I'll clean up here and then head to the *haus* to set the table. *Kinner*, go put your coats on first. You might want to wear one, too, Levi." She had a saucy grin.

Levi looked at his arms as if they didn't belong to him: he'd been so panicked when he discovered the house was empty he'd left his coat hanging in the mudroom. "*Jah*, I'll do that," he said sheepishly, although by then he hardly needed a coat, he was warm from blushing so hard.

Chapter Five

After they'd all finished eating pizza, Sadie washed the dishes while Levi gave the children baths and tucked them into bed. It wasn't until he came downstairs again that she realized she'd forgotten to talk to him about getting groceries for their Thanksgiving meal since they weren't going to Maria's house tomorrow. She offered to either stay with Elizabeth and David at the house or go to the supermarket herself, but Levi declined.

"It's late and I wouldn't want you out on the roads when there's so much traffic. The local residents are careful for buggies, but at this time of year a lot of people visit from out of state and they aren't used to sharing the road. Besides, you said you baked a pie—that's what the *kinner* want most. And I do, too."

Sadie was too embarrassed to tell him both pies were pumpkin. With nutmeg. "But there's hardly anything to eat in the pantry. If you hadn't suggested pizza tonight, I was just going to make macaroni and cheese."

"Thanksgiving is meant to be about giving thanks, not about eating. Don't worry about us. You deserve a day off with your friends."

Levi's comment caught Sadie off guard. "My friends? What friends?"

"I thought you were going to celebrate Thanksgiving with people you met at the *hochzich*," Levi said awkwardly. She had forgotten all about saying she didn't want to spend Thanksgiving with him.

"*Neh*, I didn't have any plans to spend the day with anyone else. I, um… I just didn't want to feel like a third wheel," she confessed, avoiding his eyes as she wiped an imaginary spill from the countertop with a dishcloth.

"A third wheel?"

Sadie hung her head and played with the cloth. She might as well confess it. It wasn't as if she was saying *she* wanted Levi to court *her*. "I thought you were interested in courting Maria and I didn't want to feel like I was…in the way or something."

Levi cocked his head as if considering her comment and then spoke slowly. "Maria is a *gut* friend. She and Leora were very close and she helped a lot with the *kinner* whenever my *mamm* needed. And she was a comfort to me when my *mamm* died. In some ways, I'm closer to her than I am to my own sister-in-law. But if I were interested in courting someone, it wouldn't be Maria," he said.

What does he mean by if he were interested in courting someone?

With a droll laugh, Levi said, "I assumed you wanted to spend Thanksgiving with Jonathan."

"*Neh!* I'd rather go *hungerich*!" Sadie clamped her hand over her mouth. That was an ungenerous remark but it didn't seem to faze Levi. The corners of his mustache twitched as he appeared to fight a grin.

"You *will* go *hungerich* if you join us for Thanksgiving dinner," he warned. "But we'd *wilkom* your company."

"There's nowhere I'd rather be," Sadie replied, finally meeting Levi's eyes.

It was true, too, although that didn't mean she wasn't lonesome for her family. The next morning Sadie walked to the phone shanty to call Cevilla at their agreed-upon time. As she listened to her stepmother describing Rebekah's wedding, she realized how much had changed in the short time she'd been away. How much *she* had changed. It didn't trouble her at all to hear about how, in addition to the cakes her family and guests supplied, Rebekah had ordered a specialty three-tiered lemon-raspberry cake. And she giggled as Cevilla complained that Sadie's father had nodded off during the ceremony and when she gave him a nudge, he'd jerked to attention, nearly falling out of his chair.

Then it was Sadie's turn to describe what life in Maine was like and how she was getting along in her new job. She couldn't get the words out fast enough. "The *kinner* are very sweet and my days fly by. Maine is beautiful, although it's freezing here. We might even get snow today, which is what Elizabeth and David are hoping for. But Levi doesn't want it to snow too much because he's concerned it will keep people off the roads tomorrow. That's the first day the farm opens to customers. Oh, and guess what—some of the Amish men here wear mustaches!"

"*Neh!*"

"*Jah!* Levi has one and at first it was distracting, but now I think it makes him look handsome," Sadie blurted out.

Fortunately, her brothers were with Cevilla and they

must have kept her from hearing Sadie's remark, because all she replied was, "Uh-oh, it looks as if someone else is coming to use the phone. We should give them a turn. But first your *brieder* want to wish you a happy Thanksgiving."

Sadie's younger brothers called out their greetings in the background and Sadie echoed their sentiments. Suddenly she didn't want to get off the phone, but she knew Cevilla needed to go home and continue her meal preparations, so they said their goodbyes.

On the way back to the *daadi haus*, Sadie hugged her arms around her chest. Her coat was too flimsy for this weather and she was chilled to the bone. Chilled and hungry; she was fasting until dinner, the way the Amish in Little Springs always did. To take her mind off her physical discomfort, she read Scripture and prayed for most of the morning and then curled up on the sofa in a quilt. Reclining there, she listed ten things she was thankful for in her diary, just as she did every year.

Faith in Christ.

Salvation through God's grace.

Family.

My own health and the good health of those I love.

Church family.

Provisions for all my physical needs.

The opportunity to live on a Christmas tree farm in Maine.

Satisfying work.

Elizabeth, David and Levi.

Hope.

Sadie closed her diary and thought about that last item: hope. It was no coincidence it immediately followed Levi's name. Despite her best efforts—or at least despite her initial intentions—to push all notions of romance and courtship from her mind, she had the tiniest glimmer of hope something might develop between Levi and her.

"*Kumme*, Elizabeth and David. Put those cushions back on the sofa. Sadie will be here any minute," Levi said, folding the quilt the children had draped over a set of chairs to make a cave for themselves. "She's our special guest today, so we need to show her how thankful we are she came to Maine to take care of you."

Elizabeth emerged from beneath the quilt with her nose wrinkled. "What's that *schtinke*?"

"I'm melting butter for the noodles."

"It smells really bad, Daed. I think it's burning."

Levi darted into the kitchen. Elizabeth was right: the bottom of the pot was already scorched. He removed it from the element and placed it in the sink. He'd clean that later. Then he took a new pot from the cupboard and measured a third of a cup of butter into that and turned the gas to low. "Elizabeth and David, please *kumme* in here and set the table," he called, just as Sadie rapped on the door.

"Sadie's here!" David charged past him.

Elizabeth and Levi followed him to the mudroom to welcome Sadie. "May I take your coat?" he asked awkwardly, still holding a spoon in his hand.

"*Denki*, but I'll hang it up right here. It smells like something might be burning." Sadie bent to unlace her boots.

"*Neh*, that's from before," Elizabeth said. "Daed's making dinner."

Straightening, Sadie looked into Levi's eyes. "Really? You're cooking? I thought I'd scrape together a meal."

Recalling what she'd said about girls liking to run and jump and climb, Levi gave her arm a little nudge. "Just because I'm a *bu* doesn't mean I can't cook."

Sadie's teeth were small and pretty and her eyes squinted into upside-down smiles when she laughed. "That's true. I only meant I thought I was cooking."

"*Neh*, today you're our special guest because we're thankful you came to watch us," David told her. "All the other nannies left."

Elizabeth sniffed the air. "That *schtinke* is getting worse."

Levi dashed back to the stove; sure enough, he'd burned the butter again. Sadie joined him at the sink. Surveying the pots, she asked, "Are you sure—"

"I'll get it right this time," he promised, coughing. The air was acrid. "I'm going to crack the windows in here for a couple of minutes. Please have a seat in the living room."

"You can *kumme* into our cave with us," David invited.

"*Neh*. Put those cushions back on the sofa for Sadie," he called. "Dinner will be on the table in a few minutes."

It actually took forty minutes and two more pots before Levi led them in a prayer of Thanksgiving. When they lifted their heads, he said, "Our blessings are abundant even if our food isn't."

"I'm so *hungerich* from fasting I could eat a moose," Sadie claimed, accepting the plate of buttered noodles with steamed broccoli on the side.

"Can we close the windows now? I'm cold," Elizabeth grumbled.

As soon as Levi took his first bite he apologized, "*Ach!* I didn't boil the noodles long enough."

"What are you talking about? They're fine," Sadie said, lifting a forkful to her mouth. There was discernible crunching as she chewed.

Levi rose and reached for her plate. "You don't have to eat that, really."

"Do *I* have to eat mine, Daed?" David asked.

"You do if you want pie," Sadie answered for Levi. "It's only the ends that are crunchy, so we can cut those off. That happens to me, too, if I don't push the noodles all the way down into the water."

"It's cold in here, Daed. Can we shut the windows?" Elizabeth repeated.

"Enough! I'll close the window but I want you to stop whining and eat your meal." Even though Levi had known their dinner wouldn't be lavish, he'd hoped it would turn out better than this and he was frustrated.

He strode to the window, pushed it shut and then returned to the table as Sadie wordlessly cut the ends off Elizabeth's noodles and handed her plate back to her. Noticing Elizabeth was on the brink of tears and David wouldn't meet his eyes, Levi regretted his sharp tone, but he didn't know how to lighten the mood. The only sound in the room was the *crunch, crunch, crunch* of Sadie chewing her half-cooked pasta, and before he knew it, Levi started to chortle. Soon he was shaking with a belly laugh and the children joined him. The three of them slapped the table and held on to their sides, but Sadie primly dabbed the sides of her lips with her napkin.

"What's *voll schpass*?" she asked in between crunches, which made them laugh even harder.

"Your noodles are noisy!" Elizabeth exclaimed.

"They're the noisiest Thanksgiving noodles I ever heard!" David declared, nearly spilling his milk.

"I'm sure I don't know what you're talking about. Other than the fire cracking in the living room, I don't hear a thing," Sadie said, winking at Levi. He reflexively winked back. *It's only a friendly gesture*, he told himself although he savored their playfulness.

"It's a *gut* thing Sadie made dessert. My stomach is still growling," he told the children when everyone finished eating.

"*Jah*, but she made pumpkin pie with nutmeg, Daed. You don't like—"

Levi raised an eyebrow, willing his daughter to be quiet, and to his relief she took the hint. "You're right, Elizabeth. I don't like to be the only one eating pie. Did you make it with pecans and caramel or plain, Sadie?"

Sadie furrowed her brows. "Actually, I made both kinds, but—"

"Great! I'm going to have a slice of each. But first the *kinner* and I will clean up in here and then I'll put on a pot of tea. Please go relax in the living room," Levi suggested.

Sadie tried to insist on helping, but Levi wouldn't hear of it. He rose and escorted her into the living room, where she settled onto the sofa while he stoked the fire with fresh logs and the children brought her a lap quilt.

"*Denki*," she said, leaning back against a cushion. Her cheeks were rosy and her eyes reflected the warm lamplight. "If you keep treating me like this, I'll never want to leave."

"See, Daed, I told you if you were real nice she would stay here longer," David reminded his father.

The possibility made Levi catch his breath. *If only.*

Sadie giggled to herself as she listened to the clatter of dishes and the scraping of chairs as Levi and the children cleared the table and swept the floor in the next room. There must have been half a dozen pots in the sink when there should have been only two or three. It was true the butter was burnt—even after his third attempt at melting it—and the noodles were undercooked, but Sadie didn't mind. After all, Levi was going to eat not one but two slices of pie he detested, just to be polite. What were a few lousy meals between friends?

She was so cozy lounging there that she closed her eyes and allowed her imagination to roam. David's comment about her staying longer hadn't gone unnoticed. If she and Levi had more time together, might a romantic relationship develop between them? What would it be like to kiss a man with a mustache?

"Are you having a *gut* dream?" Elizabeth asked softly and Sadie's eyes popped open. "You were smiling with your lips like this." The child pursed her lips into a half smile, half pucker.

Mortified, Sadie questioned, "Is it time for pie and tea?"

"*Jah.* Daed said to ask what kind of pie you want."

"I'd like a piece with caramel and pecans on it, please."

Elizabeth's eyes lit up. "Same as me." She skipped out of the room and returned with a plate of pie, which she set on the coffee table in front of Sadie. Then she left and came back with another plate, but this one held a plain piece of pie, as well as a piece with pecans and caramel; she set the dish next to Sadie's. *That means Levi will be sitting next to me!* Sadie felt as giddy as a schoolgirl at the idea.

When Elizabeth returned the final time, David was with her and they each held their own plates of pie, followed by Levi, who balanced a tray of teacups. The children sat on the floor on the opposite side of the coffee table and Levi seated himself next to Sadie. After pouring them both a cup, he waited for Sadie to try her pie before heartily digging into his. She was so touched by his courtesy she resisted the urge to tell him it wasn't necessary to pretend he liked the dessert.

Just as they finished, David bounced up and pointed to the window. "It's snowing!"

The white flakes were barely discernible, but Elizabeth repeated, "Snow! Look, snow! Let's go build a snowman."

"We might have to wait until it piles up to do that. How about if we go out and play Freeze Tag instead. Your *daed* has never played."

"Not it!" Elizabeth and David shouted simultaneously.

"Not it!" Sadie repeated before Levi had any idea what was happening. The children darted toward the mudroom.

"I guess that means I'm it," he sighed exaggeratedly, collecting the plates.

"*Jah*, and you'll be it for a long time if you run as slowly as you call 'not it,'" Sadie teased as she held out the tray for him to stack the dishes on.

"Oh, you're going to be the first one I catch, you

little *schnickelfritz*, you!" he warned, following her into the kitchen.

Over her shoulder she taunted, "In case you've forgotten, I have seven *brieder* and I can still outrun them all."

Levi's voice deepened as he came up beside her. "And in case *you've* forgotten, I'm not one of your *brieder*." He was flirting. They *both* were flirting. And she had no inclination to stop.

The teacups vibrated against the saucers on the tray as Sadie fought to keep her hands from trembling. When Levi spoke his breath puffed against her ear and cheek. She knew what this internal quivery feeling meant and no matter what her head told her about not falling for him, her heart spoke louder.

So did Elizabeth. "Daed! Sadie! Are you almost ready?"

Levi nearly leaped backward, causing Sadie to titter nervously. She set the tray on the counter near the sink, wiped her hands on her apron and turned to face Levi before calling, "*I'm* ready, but I don't know if your *daed* is."

She'd meant it playfully, as a reference to his ability to outrun her. But as soon as the words left her mouth she realized they sounded fraught with innuendo, as if she were questioning his readiness to be in a romantic relationship. Or was she just imagining it sounded that way because of how *she* felt? Levi probably didn't give her response a second thought.

"Be patient, please," he replied to Elizabeth while holding Sadie's gaze, which only confused the matter all the more. Was he really speaking to his daughter or was he asking Sadie to wait for him to be ready to be in a relationship?

You're hearing what you want to hear, she told herself as she pulled her coat from the peg in the mudroom. *Unless he tells you directly that he wants to court you, you have to assume he doesn't.*

"Please wear my coat, Sadie. It's too big for you to wear alone but you can put it on over yours and it should fit. Otherwise you're going to be too cold. I have another one I can wear."

"Oh, sure, you're just trying to slow me down with extra layers," Sadie joked. "*Denki,* but *neh.* After a few minutes of running around, I'll be so warm I'll need to unzip my coat."

Levi wouldn't be dissuaded, however. Without touching her, he encircled Sadie with his arms, holding the coat behind her so she had no choice but to slide her arms into it. The sleeves hung past her wrists and the wool collar was scratchy against her chin, but Levi was right—it was much warmer than hers.

"The porch is home base, Daed. If you're there you're safe and no one can tag you," David explained as they all went outside. "But you can only stay on it for the count of ten."

Elizabeth added, "And remember what we told you— the people who aren't it can unfreeze someone by tagging them."

Levi clarified, "What if I freeze all of you and there's no one left to unfreeze you?"

"Then you win and you get to pick someone else to be it," Sadie said. "But if all three of us make it back to home base at the same time, you have to be it again."

Sadie, Elizabeth and David paced across the lawn

to the fence, which was considered the starting point. Levi charged at Sadie and she shot across the yard so quickly he gave up and veered toward David, who managed to zigzag out of his way. Sadie laughed as she watched Elizabeth jump just out of his reach, too; clearly he was allowing his children to escape him on purpose, but he didn't extend her the same allowance. After gaining ground on her, he successfully faked his intended direction, causing her literally to run into his arms. They both stumbled backward from the force of the collision, but Levi grabbed Sadie by the arms to keep her upright.

"Daed, this is tag only. No fair holding on to the person," Elizabeth admonished from the safety of the porch.

Levi loosened his grip. "I'm so sorry. Are you okay?"

Sadie doubled over, using the pause to her advantage to catch her breath. Before she could assure him she was fine, David yelled, "I'll unfreeze you Sadie!" and zipped across the lawn, tagged Sadie's back and darted toward home base. She followed on his heels, arriving at the porch before Levi even realized she'd left. Only then did Sadie realize he was stunned with worry. He must have really thought he'd hurt her and she regretted scaring him.

But then Elizabeth hollered, "*You're* not the one who's supposed to freeze, Daed!" and Levi's face cracked into a gigantic grin.

"You all have until the count of ten to get off home base!" he warned. "And then I'm tagging you all."

He did, too, but Sadie didn't mind. In fact, she liked the thrill of being pursued by Levi until, breathless and laughing, he finally caught her.

* * *

"One more time, please?" David wheedled.

"*Neh*, it's getting too dark. Sadie, would you mind taking them in while I milk the cow?"

"Of course not. I'll put on a kettle for hot chocolate."

"Can we have pie, too?" Elizabeth begged.

Ordinarily Levi would tell her she'd had enough, but considering there was virtually nothing else to eat in the house, he agreed. As he milked the cow and fed the horse, he contemplated when they'd get to the grocery store. Customers were prohibited from venturing into the rows of trees at dusk—Levi didn't want them to have an accident or get lost in the dark—but a couple of nights a week he intended to keep the small lot of precut trees open until eight o'clock for the convenience of *Englisch* customers who worked until early evening.

Knowing how rambunctious the twins could be, Levi was hesitant to send them and Sadie into town, where they'd have to deal with inconsiderate tourists and their bad driving. He supposed Maria could manage the twins while tending to customers—until he remembered she might be too sick to come to work for the next few days.

Latching the heavy barn door into place, Levi prayed, *Dear Gott, please show me how to manage the needs of my business, as well as of my* familye. As he started toward the house, he saw a buggy coming up the driveway. If he wasn't mistaken, it was the deacon, Abram, and his wife, Jaala. Levi waited until they came to a stop and disembarked. Jaala was holding a platter, which she handed to Levi so she could carry one of the two coolers Abram pulled from the back of the carriage. They explained they'd heard Maria and her mother were sick, so they'd paid them a visit and Maria had told them about canceling Thanksgiving dinner at her house at the last minute.

"We brought you leftovers—unless you've already eaten," Jaala said, trailing him into the house.

Levi was overjoyed at how the Lord had answered his prayer. When he went inside and announced the news, he knew the children were less excited—they were looking forward to eating pie for supper—but he was pleased they hid their disappointment well, not uttering a word of protest.

"You brought enough to feed us for three days!" Sadie exclaimed as she helped Jaala unpack the coolers.

"We know the farm is opening tomorrow and we figured you might be too busy to get to the market."

"*Denki*. This is very generous of you. You'll sit down and join us, *jah*?" Levi asked.

"We'd like to but we're on our way to see the Zook *familye*. They came down with the twenty-four-hour bug Maria and her *mamm* had, too," Abram explained. "Ah, I almost forgot. Maria is already feeling better and she said to tell you she'll see you bright and early tomorrow morning."

Again Levi was amazed by how the Lord had answered his prayer before he'd even prayed it. "That's *wunderbaar*."

"We'll *kumme* again when we can stay longer," Jaala said as Levi escorted his visitors out the door and onto the porch. "We want to spend more time with you before you move back to Indiana."

Levi winced. He hoped the children hadn't overheard Jaala's remark. To his relief, when he went back into the kitchen, they were busily setting the table and Sadie was sliding a pan into the oven. Her eyes were gleaming when she glanced up and said, "Jaala even brought a couple of slices of apple pie. I'll save those for you, since each of the *kinner* practically have an entire pie each for themselves."

But once Elizabeth and David finished eating their meal they were too full and tired for dessert. All that running around in the fresh air had tuckered them out and they could barely pull themselves from their chairs. Before taking them upstairs to bed, Levi prompted the twins to say good-night to Sadie.

David twirled, ran to where Sadie was standing and wrapped his arms around her legs. When she bent to his level, he let go and gave her a kiss on the cheek. Not to be outdone, Elizabeth edged her way in to embrace Sadie's neck and kiss her other cheek.

"That was the happiest day I ever had," David said.

"*Jah*, and it's not even Grischtdaag," Elizabeth chimed in.

Sadie gave each of them a kiss atop their heads. "I couldn't have asked for a more *wunderbaar* Thanksgiving myself."

Levi knew what all three of them meant. "Me, neither," he said.

Chapter Six

I can't get my hopes up, Sadie wrote in her diary after she returned home from Levi's house. But it didn't matter; her hopes were already up. And why wouldn't she be hopeful after the way Levi treated her all day, cooking for her, enveloping her in his coat, even pretending to enjoy her pie? Not to mention calling her a *schnickelfritz* when they bantered in the kitchen.

That's not the kind of thing an employer says to an employee; it's the kind of thing a man says when he's being flirtatious with a woman. Sadie chewed the end of her pen before continuing. *I'm not suggesting he wants to begin a courtship with me, but who knows what might happen the more time we spend together? For now, it's just fun being around him. I can't wait for tomorrow!*

The next day she deliberately arrived at Levi's house fifteen minutes early to make him a hearty breakfast from the leftovers—mashed potato pancakes and a turkey frittata—in case he was too busy with opening-day activities to stop for lunch. It was so cold out that when Sadie inhaled through her nose it felt as if her nostrils would freeze shut, and she quickened her pace.

"Can we *kumme* to opening day, Daed?" Elizabeth asked at breakfast as she helped herself to a second potato pancake.

"You can't *go* to opening day," David told her. "Opening day is a day and we're already in it."

"I know *that*." Elizabeth was clearly indignant her brother was the one correcting her for a change. "But can I, Daed?"

"I don't want you or David anywhere near the parking lot. There will be cars coming in and out all day." Levi put down his index finger, which he'd been pointing at them. "I have to leave now, but if Sadie says it's okay, you can *kumme* to the workshop at seven forty-five. That's when everyone on the crew will gather to ask for the Lord's blessings on our work."

"Of course we'll join you there. And rest assured, I'll keep the *kinner* far away from the action," Sadie agreed.

"It's fine if you visit Maria in the workshop or visit us out by the trees. You can take the *kinner* to any of your usual spots to play, too…just as long as they're not anywhere near the parking lot."

I must really like him, Sadie thought. *Otherwise I'd tell him I heard him the first time he said that!* Instead she suggested, "It can't be more than twenty degrees out, so you'd better bundle up extra warm today."

"Twenty degrees? I'm going to leave my wool coat for you, otherwise you'll freeze," Levi's altruism snuffed out any flicker of annoyance Sadie felt at him. She insisted that since he'd be outside all day, he'd need his heavier coat and convinced him she'd grab an extra sweater at the *daadi haus* if she planned to stay out for any length of time.

Don't read too much into his offer. The niggling

thought quickly tempered her bliss. *He might just be being considerate of you because you're his employee. Remember what you thought about the diary Harrison gave you?*

Shortly after Levi left, the trio tromped down to the workshop, where Sadie gave Maria a hug. She had arrived early that day in anticipation of their first customers. "How are you doing today?" Sadie asked her.

"*Gut*. I started feeling better yesterday morning and then I regretted not having you all over for dinner."

Levi, who was standing nearby, replied, "We're glad you rested. You'll need your energy today."

Once again, Sadie was aware he was always concerned about his employees' well-being because everything had to run smoothly on the farm. As much as she wanted to, she couldn't take his kindness or attentive remarks too personally.

When the last of the crew arrived, everyone squeezed into the workshop, formed a circle and clasped each other's hands so Levi could lead them in prayer. Since Sadie was standing next to him, he reached for her hand, and she wished she had taken off her gloves first so she could have felt his touch.

"Gott, please keep us and our customers safe today," Levi requested. "Help us to serve them well for Your glory. Amen."

He didn't have to be so brief. Sadie reluctantly relaxed her fingers, releasing his hand.

"As long as we're all together, I want to say *denki* for everyone's help. Each of you plays an important role in the farm's success," Levi announced.

"Even Elizabeth and me?" David piped up, causing everyone to chuckle.

"*Jah*, we made the ornaments," Elizabeth reminded him right before someone knocked on the windowpane.

"I think that's our first customer!" Levi rubbed his hands together. "Time to get to work!"

"*Get* to work? We've *been* working," Scott ribbed him as the men filed out the door.

Before it closed behind them, Sadie could hear the Englischer asking whether the trees were organic, and then the sound of gravel popping as another car or truck rolled up the driveway. Since she knew how concerned Levi was about the children around *Englisch* vehicles and because she didn't want to be in Maria's way, Sadie said goodbye and summoned the children to accompany her to the house, promising they could go back outside once the sun had been shining long enough to bring the temperature up a few degrees.

But Elizabeth and David weren't about to miss out on any of the activities; the two of them pushed chairs to the windows so they could watch the comings and goings of the *Englisch* customers. And after completing her household chores, Sadie joined them there herself, as intent on catching sight of Levi at work as the children were.

Despite the frigid weather, customers were turning out in droves to purchase trees. Levi had expected to feel lonely for his departed wife, knowing how much she would have enjoyed opening day, but he was so busy all he felt was an urgency to keep up with the commotion. He and his crew were stationed throughout the farm to help customers with whatever they needed, whether finding the species they wanted, shaking needles off the trees and baling them, or helping strap them onto car roofs, if necessary. Although it was apparent the business was understaffed and Levi would be glad when Otto arrived the following day, all of his planning was paying off and he was grateful the other young men and Maria were such diligent employees.

Not to mention how grateful he was for Sadie. Whenever he was near enough, Levi glanced toward the house to see if she and the children were playing outdoors, but it appeared they were staying inside. Maybe she was too cold. *I should have insisted she take my coat.* Levi could have walked around in a short-sleeved shirt and still felt sweaty from all the adrenaline coursing through his body. Opening day was finally here and if the first couple of hours were an indication, sales were going strong!

"Do you have any carts?" a woman asked halfway through the morning. "We cut our tree down but we're having trouble carrying it."

On Walker's advice, Levi had invested in several carts designed for the purpose of transporting the trees, but it appeared they were all in use. Levi offered to give her a hand, so the woman led him to where her two teenage daughters were waiting beside a fallen balsam. He took the heavy end near the stump and directed them to lift the end toward the tip of the tree. They moved clumsily and slowly through the aisle. Levi considered pulling it to the baler by himself, but he preferred not to drag the trees on the ground for fear of damaging the boughs.

"Thanks," the woman said after they neared the area where customers lined up waiting for two of Levi's staff to feed trees through the baler. "This is our first Christmas since my husband died and I'm realizing all the things he did for us that I took for granted. Sometimes I don't think I deserved a man who was so good to me. If I could do things over, I'd do them completely differently."

Unsure how to respond, Levi told her he was glad to help and then excused himself and jogged across the parking lot to where Scott and a customer were struggling to align a tree across the roof rack of a small sedan.

But the stranger's disclosure touched a nerve, and hours later Levi was still ruminating on her remarks. Like the widow, Levi felt he hadn't deserved such a good spouse and he wished he would have done things differently in his marriage, too. As he was thinking about Leora, it occurred to him he'd crossed a line by entertaining Sadie alone the previous day—not because their behavior had been inappropriate, but because socializing and playing games with her and the children like that gave rise to daydreams about a romantic relationship. *Sadie's my nanny, not a replacement for my wife*, he said to himself. *I probably got carried away because being playful with her made me nostalgic about happier times with Leora. I'm not really longing for romance in the present—I'm reminiscing about the past.* Still, since he wanted to keep his emotions in check, Levi decided he'd better limit the time he spent with Sadie. And since they were so busy on the farm, he figured he'd start by skipping lunch that afternoon.

By one thirty, Sadie concluded Levi wouldn't be coming in for lunch. She'd given Elizabeth and David their meal already, and even though they hadn't spent any time outdoors, the excitement of the day had worn them out and they were getting cranky.

"After you take a little nap, we'll go outside," she promised as they headed upstairs. She came back down and was about to refrigerate the leftovers when a loud banging rattled the door. *Is that an* Englisch *customer? They're so brash—this is clearly a private* haus*, not part of the tree farm...*

But the dark, stocky man on the porch was wearing a brimmed hat. "Hello. I'm Otto, Levi's brother-in-law."

Nonplussed, Sadie opened the door wider. "I'm Sadie. Levi's out on the farm, but *kumme* in."

"*Denki.* Something smells *appenditlich*," he hinted.

"It's Thanksgiving leftovers and they're still warm. Why don't you put your suitcase in the living room and I'll fix you a plate?"

Otto popped into the other room and back into the kitchen again, sliding into a chair at the table before Sadie had a chance to turn around. "You probably weren't expecting me. I wasn't supposed to arrive until tomorrow, but on short notice our driver decided he needed to leave right after his Thanksgiving dinner and we drove straight through the night, so here I am. Looks like it's a *gut* thing, too. There were so many cars lined up outside I asked to be dropped off at the end of the road."

Sadie smiled, pleased that sales were good. "*Jah*, the farm has been buzzing all day. Levi will be glad you've arrived early. The *kinner* are upstairs taking a nap. They'll be happy to see you, too."

"I'll be happy to see *them*," Otto replied. "It's been over a year—that's far too long in between visits. My *mamm* and *schweschder* can't wait to take care of Elizabeth and David. They never wanted Levi and Leora to move to Maine in the first place. They thought the location was too remote and the community was too small." He ground pepper over the generous portion of potpie Sadie had served him.

She found herself defending Levi and Leora's decision. "Perhaps, but it's beautiful here and the farm is thriving. I think the community will grow, too."

Otto shrugged. "It probably will, but even if it doesn't, I don't share my *familye*'s opinion about Levi and my *schweschder* moving here. I'm like Leora— always up for an exciting new endeavor. And you're right about it being beautiful here. I've never seen so many pines."

"*Jah*, and yet the Englischers still *kumme* to a farm for their Grischtdaag trees," Sadie said, causing Otto to chuckle. "Would you like dessert? We have pie."

"Apple, I hope?"

Sadie had been saving Jaala's pie for Levi but it appeared as if he'd already had a slice last night after she went home, so she served Otto the remaining piece with the cream she'd freshly whipped in anticipation of Levi's return, before taking a seat at the table again.

"You look kind of old to be a nanny. Not that you look old, but you're not a schoolgirl," he commented, giving her a once-over.

Sadie didn't know exactly what he was implying but his remark ruffled her feathers all the same. "*Neh*, I'm definitely not a schoolgirl, but I'm not exactly elderly, either."

"*Ach!* I didn't mean to be offensive. I was expecting a younger nanny, that's all. But I guess in such a small community there aren't too many young *meed*."

"I don't live here. I'm from Pennsylvania," Sadie said and then wished she could take the information back. It would inevitably lead to questions about what happened to Levi's other nannies and she didn't want to cast him in a bad light. She felt protective of him. "My stepmother is distantly related to Levi, so when we heard he needed help, I decided to *kumme* for the season."

"Won't your *familye*—or your suitor—miss you during Grischtdaag?"

"I don't have a suitor and my *familye* won't miss me because I'll be going home on Grischtdaag Eve." Again, Sadie immediately regretted divulging such personal information. She abruptly stood and crossed the room to rinse a glass, her back toward Otto. Why did everyone have to mention a suitor? No wonder she was always thinking about walking out with a man—even people who'd just met her brought up the topic. Well, if Otto could ask her such an intrusive question, she could ask him, too. She set the glass upside down in the drying rack and turned to face him. "Won't your *familye* or your girlfriend miss *you* for Grischtdaag?"

"My *familye* will see plenty of me soon enough." Otto paused before admitting, "As for a girlfriend, I don't have one. Yet. But maybe I'll have one soon."

Sadie smiled in spite of herself. As unusual as it was to discuss courting with a man she'd just met, it felt good to hear someone Otto's age admit both that he wasn't walking out with anyone and also that he hadn't given up hope, either.

Eventually, Levi's hunger won out over his resolve to avoid Sadie. When he entered the house, he heard laughter that didn't sound like Sadie's coming from the other side of the mudroom door. It almost sounded like a man's, like—

"Otto!" he exclaimed. His brother-in-law wasn't supposed to arrive until the next day, and while Levi could sure use his help, it bothered him that Otto was sitting there in his kitchen, laughing with Sadie. Otto rose and they clasped each other's shoulders in a brief embrace.

"I arrived early and Sadie was kind enough to feed me. We were just discussing courting." Levi's mouth dropped open before Otto corrected himself, "I mean, the fact neither of us is courting."

Otto had always been forthright, but Levi was surprised Sadie would discuss such a topic with a virtual stranger. *He* never even broached that subject with her. Levi peeked in her direction. She was leaning against the counter with her head dipped, but Levi noticed her ears were pink. Was she embarrassed to have been caught talking about the subject with Otto? Or did the subject itself make her uncomfortable?

"I came up here for a quick lunch myself. After I eat, I'll show you around. We can sure use the help."

"Oh, *neh*, I gave the last of the meal to Otto," Sadie apologized. "Since it was nearly two o'clock, I thought you decided to skip lunch today."

"That's all right. I'll have a slice of apple pie instead."

"Otto just finished the rest of the apple pie. Would you like pumpkin?" said asked feebly.

"*Neh*. I don't like—" Levi's response was quicker and gruffer than he intended, but he stopped short of expressing his distaste for pumpkin pie. "I don't like taking it from David or Elizabeth. They're thrilled they each have the kind of pie they like for themselves. I'll eat peanut butter spread on *brot*."

"I didn't make *brot* this morning—I was out of yeast."

"Great," Levi muttered. His hunger was making him agitated and the fact Sadie had given his lunch to Otto wasn't helping matters. "Do we have enough food for dinner tonight?"

"*Jah*, I'm making soup," Sadie replied, her chin in the air.

Recognizing it sounded as if he was blaming her because there was hardly anything to eat in the house, Levi tried to lighten the mood. "What kind? Stone soup?" he joked.

"Turkey," she replied through gritted teeth, and for a split second Levi thought she was referring to him, not to the soup. "We have just enough, but I'll need to purchase groceries for tomorrow. I'm happy to take the *kinner* to the market with me when they wake from their naps."

Levi said he preferred she didn't take the children out in the buggy.

"I can take you this evening, Sadie," Otto volunteered. "I have a couple of personal items I need to get, too. The *Englisch* stores will be open late because it's Black Friday."

"That also means there will be a lot of traffic. I'm not sure I want you and Sadie going out in it," Levi protested.

"We're not *kinner*," she snapped, hands on hips.

Levi rubbed his forehead. Coming to the house was a mistake. "You're also not used to the way Englischers drive around here."

"I assume they drive just like the Englischers in Pennsylvania do—on the right side of the road. But if you're concerned about your buggy getting wrecked, I'll make a shopping list and you can go tonight. Otto will be here to watch the *kinner* after I leave."

Levi wasn't concerned about the buggy; he was concerned about Sadie and the children. But the last thing he wanted was his brother-in-law watching the twins alone. Otto was so reckless he probably made Sadie's brothers look timid. Yet Levi couldn't very well say that. And since Otto didn't know how to get to the market, he couldn't go on his own. Levi conceded aloud that the best solution was for Otto and Sadie to go together that evening.

"Gut," Otto said, bringing his dish to the sink. "It will give Sadie and me a chance to get to know each other better."

Somehow, that idea was nearly as unappealing to Levi as the thought of Otto watching the children on his own, but he couldn't change his mind now.

After Levi and his brother-in-law left, Sadie threw her energy into making up the bed for Otto, silently ranting as she worked. *What did Levi expect? Was I supposed to pull food from thin air? I'm stretching every morsel as it is. If it weren't for Jaala, we wouldn't be eating anything but scrambled* oier *today. I understand he's concerned about traffic, but sometimes his fears are just plain* lecherich.

Not that she especially wanted to go to the supermarket with Otto; he seemed pushy. No, not really pushy, but…brazen. But maybe his presence would be good for Levi. Otto wouldn't tiptoe around Levi's qualms the way Sadie had been doing. At that moment, she couldn't recall why she thought she was ever drawn to him.

As she unfurled a quilt across the bed, David came into the room. "I dreamed I heard people talking and they were staying mean things. Then Groossmammi scolded them."

Was he woken by my tense conversation with Levi? Sometimes Sadie forgot about all of the upsetting changes the children had already been through during their young lives. "If they were saying mean things, then your *groossmammi* was right to scold them."

"And after she scolded them she said I could have a piece of pie."

"Did she really?"

David shrugged. "If I was *hungerich* she would be right to tell me that."

Sadie held on to her sides and sat on the bed laughing until Elizabeth came into the room and asked what was so funny. "We were talking about your *groossmammi*, that's all."

"I miss Groossmammi," Elizabeth said. "But you're kind of like her."

"Except her hair isn't white and she doesn't have a cane," David told Elizabeth.

"And she lets us do things Groossmammi didn't let us do. Like play Freeze Tag."

"Or like eating pie when we wake up from a nap."

"Actually, I'm not going to let you do that, either." Sadie tapped the tip of his nose. "You may have pie after supper. Guess what? There's also a surprise."

"How big is it?" David wondered. They played Twenty Questions the way Sadie taught them to until they finally figured out Otto had arrived a day early.

"Daed says we can't go out with Onkel Otto unless you or Daed is with us."

"Onkel Otto never taked care of *kinner.*"

"Maybe now that he's here, he'll get some practice," Sadie said. Was she the only person Levi trusted? Including members of his own family? On one hand, she was complimented she'd earned his confidence. On the other hand, she felt the burdensome weight of his expectations. As careful as Sadie was to mind David and Elizabeth, most children were accident-prone. Sooner or later, something would happen and she didn't want to fall from Levi's good graces when it did.

The tree lot might have closed at eight o'clock, but a few stragglers lingered fifteen minutes more. After the last car drove away, the crew put the equipment in the barn and helped Maria close the workshop and secure the day's earnings. By the time Levi and Otto returned to the house, it was twenty minutes before nine and Elizabeth and David were sound asleep. Otto slurped down three bowls of turkey soup—*three!*—and he and Sadie were out the door before Levi even finished his first helping.

Afterward, he crept upstairs to check on the children. His shoulders and back were tight from hauling and hoisting trees all day and he was exhausted, but Levi knew he wouldn't be able to fall asleep until Sadie and Otto returned. Even after he'd soaked in a hot tub, his muscles felt like they were in knots—and so did his stomach.

Why am I so uneasy? The day's tree and wreath sales far exceeded his expectations. Levi should have felt satisfaction, but he couldn't shake the feeling something was amiss. Yes, he wished Leora had been there to experience opening day, but that wasn't the only reason he felt discontent. Otto's arrival had also unsettled him. *I'll probably never get to be with just Sadie and the* kinner *again. Otto will always be with us,* he complained to himself. Just because he'd resolved to limit the amount of time he spent with Sadie didn't mean he wanted the entire dynamic of the household to change.

Once again, Levi realized too late he should have appreciated a good thing when he had it, just as the customer had said earlier that day.

Levi was right; there were a lot of crazy drivers on the road, zipping past the buggy at full speed or coming so close Sadie could have seen the whites of their eyes if it had been daytime. From what she'd overheard from *Englischers* back home, Sadie assumed Black Friday sales didn't apply to food, but there were so many shoppers in the supermarket no one would have ever known it was after nine o'clock in the evening.

Since they had a lot to purchase, she gave Otto a third of the list and shopped for the rest of the items herself. They agreed to meet at the checkout line when they finished gathering their groceries, but when Sadie arrived near the cash registers Otto was nowhere to be found. She waited for what must have been half an hour and then she finally decided to go search for him.

Up and down the aisles she roamed, growing increasingly impatient. As she rounded the dairy section, she passed two *Englisch* girls.

"Look, there's another one!" she heard the taller girl exclaim. "Get her picture."

Another one? Sadie wondered if that meant they'd seen Otto or a different Amish person in the store. She wasn't about to ask, so she averted her eyes from their

law here, he'd rather be short-staffed. "Next time, I'll go myself," he uttered.

Sadie set a can onto the counter with a clunk. "You go right ahead and do that, then. *Gut nacht*, Otto," she said before flouncing out the door.

Astonished that Sadie acted as if *he* were the one who'd done something wrong, Levi indignantly stormed off in the opposite direction, leaving Otto standing in the kitchen alone. *The least he can do is put the groceries away*, Levi thought begrudgingly. *Since he's probably going to eat most of the food himself.*

Chapter Seven

When Sadie opened the shades and saw it must have snowed six to eight inches overnight, she was delighted, despite her ugly interaction with Levi the previous evening. The mere anticipation of Elizabeth and David's jubilance made her speed through her morning routine. She layered herself with so much clothing she could hardly fasten her coat. Levi had commented the temperatures usually weren't this low this soon in the season, so Sadie hoped the cold snap wouldn't continue, otherwise she'd have to purchase a new coat.

Not only would the expenditure be unnecessary, since she'd only be staying in Maine for a short time, but in order to purchase a new coat she'd have to ask Levi to take her shopping. And right now she didn't even want to ask him the time of day. Recalling his attitude when she and Otto had returned home late, she thought, *It's not as if I wanted to go shopping in a crowded store at that time of night with a virtual stranger while being hounded by Englischers trying to photograph us! You'd think Levi would have been grateful we'd gone at all, not resentful it took us so long.*

Sadie wound her scarf around her neck and opened the door. The blast of air made her eyes sting and her skin smart. By the time she arrived at Levi's house, even her teeth were cold.

"Guess what, Sadie. Onkel Otto is here! And it snowed last night!" David announced even though Sadie was already aware on both counts. "We're going to make a snowman."

"Not in your pajamas, you aren't. Go get dressed, please. And put on clean socks, not the ones you left on the floor last night," Levi admonished from the doorway. After David scurried from the room, Levi said to Sadie, "I made *kaffi*. I'll get you a cup."

"I don't want any, *denki*," Sadie replied crisply. She did, but not if Levi thought pouring a cup of coffee would make up for how thankless he'd been the night before. She put a pot on the stove for oatmeal and a pan for bacon and eggs; Levi and Otto were probably hungry after last night's light meal and they'd need energy today. She could sense Levi shifting from foot to foot near his place at the table. Why was he watching her? She had nothing more to say to him.

"*Guder mariye*, Sadie," Otto said, sniffing as he entered the kitchen. "That smells *wunderbaar*. I'm so *hungerich* I could eat a moose."

"As it happens, that's what I'm making," Sadie jested, shooting Otto a big smile to show she wasn't upset with *him*. Then she deliberately edged around Levi to set the table, landing his plate with a plunk in front of him.

Otto chortled at her joke, oblivious to the tension between Sadie and Levi. With a glance toward the window he said, "It must be really cold out there this morning."

"Not nearly as cold as it is in here," Levi uttered so

quietly Sadie thought she might have imagined it. She didn't know whether his comment made her want to laugh or stick him with a fork.

Suddenly David and Elizabeth were upon them, their exuberance thawing the mood. "We're going to play a game outside called Cut the Pie," Elizabeth told Otto and Levi.

"It's not a real pie. It's a pie you draw in the snow and you chase each other around it."

"Sadie teaches you so many *gut* games, doesn't she?" Levi asked. "She's brought a lot of *schpass* into our lives."

Sadie deftly flipped the eggs in rapid succession. A compliment still wasn't an apology. She suggested Levi say grace but afterward she popped out of her chair again and remained on her feet, as if she were too busy serving to join the others.

"Do you know what snowshoes are?" Otto asked the children as he filled their bowls with oatmeal from the pot Sadie put on the table.

"Jah," Elizabeth said knowingly, pursing her lips to blow on her oatmeal. "They're boots a snowman wears."

To his credit, Otto didn't laugh. "Well, you're right that they're a special kind of footwear, but they're not for snowmen. People wear them so they can walk on top of really deep snow without sinking into it."

"Do you have snowshoes?" David questioned.

"Neh, but last night when Sadie and I were out I saw an *Englisch* shop where people can rent them. If the snow gets deeper, I might get some for all of us. What do you think of that?"

Levi was shaking his head. "I don't think that's a *gut* idea for the *kinner.*"

"I'll cover the costs," Otto said. "We can go right here in the yard."

"I said *neh*." Levi sounded as if he were refusing the children's request, not a grown man's.

Irritated by his tone, as well as by his suffocating safety concerns, Sadie addressed Otto. "*I'd* like to go." Then, knowing the suggestion would rattle Levi, she taunted, "Maybe if we get enough practice, we can go on one of the trails at the college. Or nearby in Stetson or Canaan. Maria told me people here sometimes rent a van and go with a group from the Unity district."

"That sounds great. I'll check into it," Otto replied.

Sadie's momentary triumph was followed by a wave of regret; she didn't really want to travel by van to a snowshoeing trail, especially not with Otto. Just because Levi had been a dolt didn't mean she had to be one, too. But there was no taking it back now.

Levi squeezed his hands into fists beneath the table. He had wanted to start today off better than yesterday ended, but he was annoyed Otto had suggested an activity like snowshoeing with the children without checking with Levi first. And it was one thing if Sadie was going to be a sourpuss to Levi, but why was she sidling up to Otto? He should have known this arrangement was a bad idea. Three adults in the house was one adult too many. Just as Levi feared would happen, Otto was upsetting the tentatively happy atmosphere he and Sadie had created.

"You'll have to go on a Sunday since the farm is open six days a week," he said.

"Obviously." Sadie glanced his way for the first time since she arrived and her eyes were as fiery as her voice.

Levi pushed his chair back. "The two of you can make your recreation plans later. Right now it's time for work. We've got to clear the walkways before the farm opens."

Otto was still spooning oatmeal into his mouth, like the bottomless pit he was. Levi bade the children goodbye in his usual way and said to Sadie, "I don't mind if they run around in the snow but—"

"But you don't want them playing anywhere near the cars. You told me—and them—already. Repeatedly," Sadie retorted. "There's nothing wrong with my ears."

Neh, but there's something wrong with your attitude, Levi thought as he yanked his coat on. Fueled by anger, he'd already carved out a path from the parking lot to the workshop by the time Otto came out to retrieve a second shovel for himself from the barn. It wouldn't be long until Scott arrived with a plow on the front of his truck to clear out the parking area, which he agreed to do whenever there was snowfall. As Levi and Otto stopped to catch their breath and watch Scott's truck push snow into high banks, Otto leaned on the handle of his shovel. He surveyed the snow, which glittered in the sunlight.

"The first year you moved to Maine, Leora wrote to Mamm telling her how much she loved winter here," Otto said.

Levi remembered. That season they'd had a record-breaking amount of snowfall, beginning in October and running until April, yet Leora had rarely skipped the opportunity to hang the laundry on the clothesline outside, instead of in the basement. The clothes would inevitably freeze so thoroughly Levi's pants could practically stand up on their own, so Leora would have to defrost them in front of the woodstove. But she claimed she loved wearing the smell of winter on her clothes, that it invigorated her.

"She said you two were considering learning to cross-country ski," Otto continued. "She loved trying new activities."

If he thinks he can twist my arm into letting the kinner *go snowshoeing by talking about Leora, he's wrong.* "That was before she had the *boblin*."

"Oh. She became more cautious after Elizabeth and David were born?"

Otto started shoveling again, not waiting for Levi's reply. Likely he knew the answer: Leora hadn't become more cautious. If anything, she became more audacious. Not that she was ever reckless—she guarded the children's safety with her life. But she was constantly talking about all the wonderful things they'd teach the children to do outdoors, for both work and play—things she'd wanted to try as a child but couldn't because their property was too small and her parents were too strict. Even so, Levi was sure that if she knew then how easily an injury could claim a life, she would have been more restrictive, too.

He walked over to set the shovel next to the workshop door in case he needed to use it again, and waved to Walker, who emerged from the barn. Just then the first customer raced up the driveway in a black SUV. Levi realized many of the Englischers had four-wheel drive but that didn't mean everyone did.

"Did you see him barreling up the driveway?" he asked when Walker reached him. "I'm going to go tell that guy he better not leave as quickly as he came in."

"If you do, he'll leave *quicker* than he came in,"

Walker frankly replied. "He wasn't going that fast and there was no one anywhere near his truck. If you go talk to him now with that attitude, you're going lose a customer and reflect poorly on our community."

Levi argued, "But I want to prevent anyone from getting hurt."

"Then put up a sign that says Please Drive Slowly. But don't ruin a relationship with a customer, as well as risk your reputation as a business owner, by holding everyone to your safety standards, especially since no one was in danger." The customer waved to Walker, who waved back, indicating he'd be right over to answer his question.

As much as Levi tried to justify his anger at the customer—and at Otto and Sadie—he realized Walker was right. Levi was perilously close to ruining relationships. Losing customers. Maybe even losing employees. Sadie, to be precise. He resolved to take her aside at lunch and apologize. But between carting trees, directing his staff and assisting an *Englisch* teenage driver who lost traction after backing into a snowbank and needed a push forward, Levi lost track of time. He wouldn't have even known it was time to eat if Otto hadn't told him what fantastic chili Sadie had made— usually they took their breaks at the same time.

"You ate already?" Levi suspected Otto had headed to the house early to be alone with Sadie.

"*Jah*, over an hour ago." Otto patted his stomach. "I would have polished everything off if Sadie hadn't stopped me. She put some aside for you and told me to tell you to heat it up if she wasn't there. She planned to take Elizabeth and David outside for a while."

Levi hiked toward the porch. Halfway between the

workshop and the house, he spotted tracks where Sadie must have played Cut the Pie with David and Elizabeth. He shaded his eyes to see an object on the snow and assumed one of the children had dropped a mitten. Then he realized it was crimson, a little pool of blood. Beyond that, a trail of droplets led to his home. Levi's stomach lurched. Was it David's or Elizabeth's? Sadie's?

He ran like a stallion and bolted through the mudroom into the kitchen just as Sadie came through from the living room. "What's wrong?" she asked.

At the same time he questioned, "Are the *kinner* okay?" Levi leaped toward the hall, but Sadie blocked his way.

"Shh. They're napping. They're fine."

Levi was nearly panting. "I saw blood in the snow."

"Oh, that," Sadie picked up a dish towel. "David had a nosebleed. It stopped before we even got inside."

"A nosebleed? How did it happen? Did he fall? Or run into someone?" Levi couldn't stop himself from accusing, "It was because of that game you taught them, wasn't it?"

"Absatz," Sadie yawped, tossing the dish towel onto the counter. "You need to calm down, Levi."

"Don't tell me to calm down. My *kind* was hurt under your care and you owe me an explanation!"

Sadie jammed her hands onto her hips and leaned forward. She drew no small measure of satisfaction from telling Levi exactly what happened. *"Neh*, he didn't run into anything and he didn't fall, nor was he hit. His nose just started to bleed. Probably because the air in the house is so dry because you turn the gas heat way up and always have a bonfire raging in the woodstove. If it's anyone's fault he got a nosebleed, it's *yours*."

Levi slumped into the couch. He looked more dazed than embarrassed, and when he finally spoke, his voice quavered. "You're right. I'm sorry for blaming you." He shielded his face with his arm, appearing so woebegone Sadie's anger melted faster than butter in a skillet. Levi moaned, "It was my fault. It was all my fault."

Perching on the cushion beside him, Sadie consoled, "It only bled a little. It probably looked worse than it was because of the contrast with the snow. It's not really your fault. I only said that because you blamed *me*." When Levi didn't respond, she gently elbowed his side. "If it's anyone's fault, it's David's. I've seen him stick his fingers in his nose. Between that and the dry air, his nasal membranes probably got irritated. My youngest *bruder* gets nosebleeds so often from picking his nose that my stepmother threatens to sew mittens onto his hands if he doesn't stop poking around in there."

Sadie wasn't sure whether the noise Levi made was a laugh or a gulp. "You don't understand. It was my fault."

Realizing he wasn't talking about David's nosebleed, Sadie urged, "What was your fault, Levi? You can tell me."

"Leora," he said, and for a moment Sadie thought he was confused, addressing her by his departed wife's name. Then she recognized he was referring to Leora's fall.

"Leora's accident was your fault?" He nodded when she said it for him. "How was that your fault? You weren't even home."

Levi dropped his arm but didn't face Sadie as he told her about neglecting to return Leora's stepladder to the house, which meant she had to use a kitchen chair to wash the windows. Sadie was aware Levi's guilt was as real to him as the floor beneath his feet, but to her it was completely unjustified. She waited until he quieted before saying, "That still doesn't make it your fault, Levi. Gott is sovereign. He ordained the number of days for each of our lives."

"I know that," Levi agreed, nodding. Yet in the next breath he contradicted himself, "But don't you see? I was part of the reason Leora's life was cut short. I made a mistake. A thoughtless, careless, self-centered mistake." His chin dropped to his chest again. It occurred to Sadie he'd likely never told anyone this secret. Levi's guilt was false guilt, but that didn't mean it didn't have a very real effect on him. In her own experience, Sadie always felt better once she confessed her guilt or wrongdoings to God.

After a quiet spell, she said, "Since you already know about Gott's will and sovereignty, I won't say anything else about that. But I wonder if you've ever considered maybe Leora's death had nothing to do with standing on a chair. Maybe she had a dizzy spell. In that case, it wouldn't have mattered whether she was standing on the stepladder, she still would have fallen."

Levi shook his head. "Not likely. She was in perfect health."

It was going to be harder to get through to him than Sadie first thought. His guilt must have taken deep root from years of living with it. Sadie was hesitant to suggest, "She might have gotten dizzy from being too *hungerich*."

"She'd just eaten. There were leftovers from her lunch in the fridge."

"Could it... Could it be possible Leora should have exercised more discretion?"

Glowering at Sadie, Levi defended his wife. "Leora didn't want to die. How can you even suggest such a thing?"

"*Neh*, of course she didn't want to die. But I've cleaned lots of windows before. I've taken shortcuts, stood on my tiptoes to reach a pane because I was too lazy or rushed to get a stepladder. Surely you've done the same thing when you've repaired your roof or helped with a barn raising. Maybe that's what happened with Leora. She made an error in judgment, that's all."

"You're saying it's her fault!" Levi jumped up, his forehead slashed with angry lines. "How dare you say it's her fault? That's *lecherich*!"

Sadie remained calm, evenly replying, "That's my point. I think if Leora were here, she'd ask how dare *you* say it's *your* fault. She'd say *you're* being *lecherich*. And whether you claim you already know it or not, I think she'd remind you what Scripture says about Gott determining the number of our days."

"What do you know about what my wife would think?" Levi's vehemence was loud enough to wake the children, but Sadie persisted.

"I know if I had a husband and I died, it would crush me to think he was bearing such a tremendous and unnecessary burden. I'd want him to let go."

"I *have* let go of my wife," Levi barked. "I know she's in Heaven with the Lord."

"I mean let go of your guilt."

Levi shook his head and stared out the window, his eyes brimming, his nostrils red.

"It's not *gut* for you. Or for your *kinner*. The Lord

doesn't want you to carry a burden that's not yours to carry."

Levi was momentarily stupefied. "I don't know how to let go," he finally rasped.

Sadie stood. "Give it to Gott," she whispered. She could hear the creak of Elizabeth's bed upstairs. Footsteps would soon follow.

Levi chewed his bottom lip, nodding. "I'm sorry for the way I spoke to you last night. And then just now, about David's nosebleed. I was… I was scared something awful had happened."

"I forgive you," she murmured. "And I understand why…"

"Why I'm such a control freak?"

Sadie chuckled. "Those are your words, not mine," she said as the patter of stocking feet on hardwood floors grew louder and the children appeared.

David sounded proud to announce, "Daed, I got a bloody nose!"

"That's because he picks it," Elizabeth said with disgust.

"You pick your nose, too," David countered.

"No pie for *kinner* who quarrel," Sadie told them.

"We get pie? Now?" Elizabeth asked.

"Sure. You may each have a slice while your *daed* eats his chili. Then he has to get back to work."

"Can we play Cut the Pie again when we're done eating our real pie, Daed?"

"If Sadie says so, then you may. She's in charge and she knows best," Levi said, looking right into Sadie's eyes. In that instant she felt as if a thousand icicles melted between them.

* * *

When Levi left the house, his stomach was full but his step was light. He would have been mortified to have broken down like that in front of anyone else, but Sadie was so sympathetic her response was healing. Levi had prayed for forgiveness for his part in his wife's accident, but he'd never thought to pray for relief from his guilt. False guilt, to hear Sadie tell it. He wasn't convinced she was right, but as he surveyed the pristine landscape, he desired for his conscience to be as white as snow, too. *Lord*, he prayed, *I know You forgive me. If it's really not my fault Leora died, please cleanse me of my guilt. And please help me to release my fears and trust You more.*

Beyond that, he didn't know what else to do, but Levi hoped the Lord would work out the details once Levi surrendered his burden to Him. He couldn't guess how long it would take or how challenging it would be to forgive himself and let go of the worries that bound him, but he was willing to try and that was a start.

The first real test of that willingness came a week later, on the first Saturday in December. After a snowfall blanketed the yard with eight more inches of powdery whiteness and the children asked if they could make an igloo, Levi hesitated, envisioning it collapsing on them, but he prayed a swift, silent prayer and then said, *"Jah."*

Sadie sweetly whispered an assurance into his ear. "We'll be careful. Don't worry."

"I won't," he said and he meant it.

Levi was grateful he and Sadie had come to a new understanding. In hindsight, he realized that until that point, it was Sadie who had been making most of the compromises in regard to his preferences for the children's activities, likely because she was his employee. Now that Levi was trying to release his fears and allowing Sadie to voice her opinions about the twins' safety, his relationship with her was more of an equal partnership and the tension between them dissipated entirely.

Adjusting to Otto's boisterous and constant presence—as well as to his voracious appetite—took a little more time. As productive and good-natured as Otto was at work, he had a tendency to monopolize conversations—and hog the food—during their family meal times. Levi would have thought anyone who talked so much wouldn't have been able to simultaneously eat so much, but somehow Otto managed. His behavior grated on Levi's nerves, and from the way Sadie sometimes pinched her lips together, he knew it was getting to her, too. But she was too gracious to say anything, so Levi tried to follow her example.

Then one morning he was struck with a realization: he and Otto should take their lunch breaks separately. That way, Levi could at least have a little peace for *one* meal of the day. Before heading out the door, he presented the idea to Sadie in private, using the legitimate excuse that it was too busy on the farm for two men to be gone at the same time. However, he wanted to make sure she didn't mind serving lunch twice.

"That's fine but I'm trying to stick to a schedule with the twins' naptime since they're outgrowing the need to sleep during the day. I like to put them down by one o'clock. They're always eager to spend time with you, so if you take your break first, you can eat with them. I'll have lunch with Otto afterward so he doesn't have to eat alone."

"Neh," Levi protested. It wouldn't be fair to subject Sadie to enduring Otto's vociferousness by herself. But Levi knew if he told her that she'd claim she didn't mind, so instead he explained, "Things are so *narrish* on the farm I'd appreciate a little quiet time in the middle of the day to get my thoughts together. How about if you serve Otto and the *kinner* first, and then you and I can eat together after that?"

Sadie cocked her head as if trying to comprehend the punch line of a joke. Did she feel uncomfortable eating alone with him? Levi didn't want her to suspect he had an ulterior motive.

"Unless you'd rather eat with my son, who puts his fingers in his nose," he quipped, making Sadie giggle. "And my daughter, who bosses everyone around."

"Don't forget your brother-in-law, who eats everything in sight. I've started hiding food from him!" She laughed again. "Hmm. It's a difficult decision, but I guess I'll eat with you."

Levi grinned. He supposed he should have felt guilty for scheming to avoid his brother-in-law, but he was too relieved he'd get to enjoy one nice, calm meal a day. As for his previous intention to limit the time he spent with Sadie, well, in this instance, it couldn't be helped. At least, that was what Levi told himself.

Sadie drew a line down the center of the page in her diary dated December 12. Ever since Levi confided in her after David's nosebleed, she felt the connection between them had deepened. However, it might have been a false sense of intimacy simply because he'd shared a personal secret with her—she couldn't be sure. So, on one side of the page she listed the reasons she thought Levi might be interested in her romantically.

He laughs at my jokes even when they aren't that funny.

He frequently says how glad he is I'm here.

He asked me to eat lunch alone with him—EVERY day of the workweek!

The way he looks at me.

Then on the other side of the page, she wrote the reasons she didn't know if he liked her. Actually, it was only one reason:

He hasn't said it in plain language.

But, she thought, *just because he hasn't said it yet doesn't mean he won't.* Considering how hesitant Levi was to take physical risks, Sadie rationalized he'd be reluctant to make himself emotionally vulnerable, too.

We don't have much time left before we part ways. Maybe he doesn't think I'd be interested in a long-distance courtship, she further reasoned. *Or he has qualms about a long-distance courtship working out.* Both excuses seemed weak. Of *course* she'd be interested in a long-distance relationship and she was confident that with a little effort the two of them could develop their relationship through letters and visits. But how could she convince Levi of that if he never brought up the topic?

Sadie sighed and set down her pen. *I'm doing it again.* If there was one thing she should have learned by now, it was that if a man didn't overtly express a romantic interest in her, it was because he wasn't romantically interested. As difficult as it was going to be, she was just going to have to try harder to quell her longing to have Levi as her suitor. *Soon enough, I'll be back in*

Pennsylvania. It'll get easier once I don't have to see him every day, she consoled herself.

A few days later, she dropped by the workshop so the twins could replenish the tree stump ornament supply and she could help assemble wreaths and visit with her friend. As she and Maria worked, they chatted about everything from Maria's mother's health to what Sadie was planning to purchase for her brothers and other family members for Christmas.

"You must miss them a lot," Maria said.

"*Jah*, but I'll see them soon." Sadie did miss her family, but she was going to miss Levi and his children when she returned home, too.

"It's a shame you have to leave. I like having you here."

"I like having her here, too." Elizabeth's comment served as a reminder that little children had big ears.

"It's too bad you can't stay," Maria repeated, her voice low.

"*Jah*, but what would I do here?" whispered Sadie. "I came to be a nanny and Levi and the *kinner* are moving to Indiana in January."

"He's only moving because he doesn't have anyone to watch the *kinner*. If you stayed permanently, he wouldn't have to move."

Sadie was so flustered by the suggestion she snipped the loop of a bow instead of the trail of ribbon. The same idea had crossed her mind once or twice before, but given how eager Otto said his parents were to care for the twins, as well as how much preparation Levi had put into their move, Sadie considered it a foregone conclusion they'd relocate to Indiana. "He hasn't asked me to stay."

"But if he did?" Maria pressed.

She shrugged. "I suppose I'd say *jah*."

"I knew it! What did I tell you about love creeping up on you?"

"Shush," Sadie warned, pointing toward the children. "Who said anything about love? I'd stay because of the *kinner*."

And because if I stayed, it would give Levi more time to ask to be my suitor. It would also mean we wouldn't have to have a long-distance courtship. Sadie tried to banish the thoughts even as they occurred to her, but it was futile: some dreams weren't so easily dismissed.

In the three weeks since Thanksgiving, the hours on the tree farm were longer, the work harder and the customers more demanding than Levi had expected, but it was all worth it because it meant he could repay the last of his property loan, even before the sale of the land and houses was finalized. He didn't want to be saddled with debt when he returned to Indiana. He wouldn't make nearly the income working in the factory or even in construction that he made working for Colin. And although he and the twins initially would live with his in-laws, as soon as he could he hoped to buy or build a house, which would be more expensive in Indiana than it was in Maine.

"If this demand keeps up for one more week, I'll be able to pay back my loan before we move," he confided to Maria one evening after they reconciled the cash box.

"Then you're really moving?" she asked.

"Why wouldn't I be?"

Maria shut the ledger. "If I can be blunt, I thought

things are working out so well with Sadie that maybe you wouldn't need to move."

"What do you mean?" Levi was immediately wary; Maria had a reputation for pushing single people together.

"Sadie's so *gut* with the *kinner*, I figured maybe she'd continue to live in the *daadi haus* and mind Elizabeth and David permanently. Then you wouldn't have to uproot the twins."

"Oh," Levi said and for an instant he felt oddly let down that Maria *hadn't* been playing matchmaker. "I haven't really given that much consideration."

Which wasn't the same as saying he'd *never* considered it. Sure, the idea had occurred to him on occasion, but only as a passing wish, not as a realistic possibility. After all, he had prospective buyers for the houses and property, and his in-laws were preparing their own home for his arrival with the twins. They'd never been in favor of Levi raising Elizabeth and David in Maine and he suspected they were relieved when none of the nannies worked out after his mother died. When Levi really thought about it, he could see their point; they were Leora's family—who better to help raise the children than them? They'd be bitterly disappointed if Levi changed his mind now.

Furthermore, Sadie had specifically committed to staying until December 24, when she'd return home to celebrate Christmas with her own family in her own community. A temporary arrangement was one thing, but Levi couldn't ask Sadie to leave *her* loved ones to care for *his* family for years to come. As much as he cherished living in Serenity Ridge, Levi recognized the small community didn't have a lot to offer a young, single woman like Sadie. *Just because I don't deserve to experience romantic love again doesn't mean Sadie should forgo—or postpone—an opportunity for courtship and marriage*, he thought ruefully.

"But now that you *have* considered it…?" Maria prompted, bringing him back to their conversation.

"You're right, I can't imagine anyone being a better nanny for the *kinner* than Sadie is. But I have no intention of changing my plans to move," Levi stated decisively.

Chapter Eight

Sadie relished her lunches alone with Levi; conversation and laughter came easily whenever they were together and Levi was attentive to every word she said. They shared anecdotes about their pasts, discussed their faith and simply enjoyed the flavor of their meals or remarked on the beauty of the snow. It almost felt as if they were walking out together. But *almost* wasn't good enough. Ever since Maria mentioned how perfect it would be if Sadie could stay in Maine, Sadie thought of little else, but time was running out. It was already December 18, the Friday before her last weekend in Serenity Ridge.

December 18—that meant Harrison and Mary had gotten married three days ago, on Tuesday the fifteenth. Sadie was delighted the day had come and gone without it occurring to her it was Harrison's wedding day. She would have expected to experience at least a tiny smoldering of bitterness, but time and distance had healed her heart and she could honestly claim she hoped their wedding was a blessed, festive occasion.

A festive occasion! That *might nudge Levi in the*

right direction. Sadie realized the most lighthearted moments she'd shared with him so far had occurred whenever they took part in a celebration, such as the wedding or the Thanksgiving holiday. She couldn't very well suggest a date or a dinner for just the two of them; that simply wasn't done. Amish women didn't ask out Amish men. But they *did* make it easier for Amish men to ask *them* to walk out. What better way to inspire Levi to ask to be her suitor—or at least to ask her to stay in Maine—than to put the two of them in a social situation together?

She chewed her pinky fingernail, considering whether or not it was reasonable to invite people to a party at such short notice. She supposed there would be at least a few people—Maria, Jaala and Abram, perhaps, and possibly Walker—who might agree to attend if they didn't already have plans or weren't traveling. But Levi worked such late hours it wasn't practical to host a party during the week. And he truly did relish a day of rest on the Sabbath.

She snapped her fingers as another idea struck her— she didn't have to throw a full-fledged party; she could invite Maria to join them for a special supper! Maria would already be on the farm, so she could come to the house after she closed the workshop for the evening. Sadie paced the room, considering whether to invite Walker, too. Although he was a widower, he had a small daughter his mother cared for during the day; perhaps they could all come. But then the tone of the party would shift more toward a family gathering, when Sadie wanted it to be a time for adults—for *couples*.

As Sadie was dithering over whom to invite, Otto lumbered through the door, asking what was for lunch.

Otto! Why hadn't she thought of this before? Sadie could match him up with Maria. *The four of us could play board games after the twins go to bed. It will be a lot of* schpass *and, who knows, maybe it will be a happy beginning for* two *couples!*

"It's baked ham salad," she replied. "The twins are washing their hands. Before they *kumme* in, I want to run something by you."

"Sure. Could I have a piece of that *brot* to eat while you're talking? I'm starving."

"You're worse than the *kinner*." Sadie laughed but sliced a thick piece from the warm loaf, slathered it with butter and gave it to Otto, who didn't bother to sit before biting into it. "I'd like to have a little get-together here. I could ask Maria to join us for supper after work on Monday evening. Once the *kinner* are in bed, the four of us can play board games and visit."

Sadie stole a glance at Otto, who was attentive but silent, his mouth full. She felt transparent, as if he could see the real reason behind the event. She added, "I suppose you, Levi and I could just hang out together, but it makes it more of a special occasion to have a guest. Besides, playing games with three people isn't nearly as much fun as pairing up in teams, right?"

Otto rubbed crumbs from his lips with the back of his hand, his eyes sparkling. "*Jah*. That sounds *wunderbaar*."

Sadie was so excited she didn't wait to ask Levi if it was okay with him. As soon as Otto and the children sat down to eat, Sadie darted to the workshop to invite Maria. If Maria suspected Sadie was matchmaking, she either didn't mind or she was she was too busy ringing up customers' purchases to notice, because she immediately accepted. Sadie dashed back to the house just in time to stop Otto from dishing a second helping of ham salad to the children and what must have been a third helping to himself.

"Ah-ah-ah," she scolded and attempted to take the serving utensil from his hand. He held fast, so she clasped his wrist with one hand and the length of the utensil with the other, pulling harder. "Levi hasn't had any yet."

Otto sighed and opened his fingers. "You're right. He won't agree to the party if he's *hungerich* and cranky."

"What party?" Elizabeth didn't miss a thing.

"It's for adults," Otto informed his niece. "No *kinner* allowed."

Elizabeth's face screwed into a pout and David asked, "Why not?"

"Because sometimes grown-ups need to spend time alone so they can get to know each other better without being interrupted by little *meed* and *buwe*, right, Sadie?"

"That's true, but—"

"We don't interrupt," Elizabeth interrupted. "If we're real quiet, can we *kumme*?"

Sadie started again, "*Jah*, you may *kumme* to the first part of the party and you may each choose one game for all of us to play before you go to bed."

"Will we have cake?" David asked.

"*Jah*, will we?" Otto echoed, cracking Sadie up. He really *was* as bad as the children.

"Sure. What kind should we have?"

"Peanut butter sheet cake," Otto promptly replied, even though Sadie had intended for the children to answer the question.

"Does everyone like peanut butter sheet cake?"

"I love it," David said.

"Me, too," Elizabeth agreed.

Sadie waited, hoping they'd mention whether Levi liked it or not, too. When they didn't, she hinted, "Peanut butter sheet cake it is, then, as long as it's okay with your *daed*." *Since when have I become so concerned about what pleases a man's appetite?*

"If he doesn't like it, I'll eat his piece," Otto suggested, rising to leave. "I might eat his piece anyway."

Sadie smirked at him, but she was so grateful he'd agreed the party was a good idea she would have made him his own cake if he asked.

Because the baler jammed and Levi had to repair it, he didn't take his break until after two o'clock. By then he could have skipped lunch and waited until supper to eat, but he didn't want to miss out on enjoying one of Sadie's delicious meals with her. Over the course of time as they met daily for lunch, Levi had let his guard down. Their afternoon mealtimes were filled with companionable conversation and warm humor, and although Levi's fondness for Sadie had deepened, he was less concerned about confusing nostalgia for his wife with his feelings toward Sadie. As their time together wound down, instead of keeping his distance, Levi found himself justifying his desire to be alone with Sadie by telling himself, *She's my friend, just as Maria is my friend.* But he couldn't quite explain to himself why he was disappointed that on that particular Friday, the children were already awake from their naps and so he couldn't enjoy a meal alone with Sadie.

"Look, Daed—" Elizabeth pointed to the window "—we decorated for Grischtdaag."

Sadie must have helped them place boughs on the mantelpiece and windowsills. In the center of each arrangement stood a tall white candle tied with a red bow. The Amish decorated their homes sparsely for Christmas, but he'd always felt the effect was beautiful. Last year his mother had only had enough energy to decorate the *daadi haus*, so Levi wasn't surprised the children were thrilled to adorn their own home this year.

He twisted his knuckles into his closed eyelids and then opened them again and rattled his head. "I've been around so many Grischtdaag trees I see them in my sleep, so when I noticed those boughs in the window, I thought my mind was playing tricks on me."

Elizabeth replied solemnly, "*Neh*, they're real, Daed."

"The candles are real, too, but we have to pretend they're burning because Sadie doesn't ever, ever, *ever* want to catch us lighting a match." David was clearly imitating Sadie's tone.

Relieved she must have issued a stern warning, Levi said, "If you're very careful not to bump them, the adults will light them for a special occasion, like Grischtdaag."

"Speaking of special occasions," Sadie began, "now that the *haus* is decorated and the season is winding down, I thought we'd have a little pre-Grischtdaag party on Monday."

Since Sadie said she'd already invited Maria and told Otto about the event, Levi couldn't refuse. Nor did he want to. For the rest of the afternoon, he was filled with jittery energy. Planning a party went above and beyond Sadie's responsibilities as an employee. *She seems to have really connected with us and with Maria. Maybe she'd be open to the idea of moving here long-term after all.* As quickly as the idea popped into Levi's mind, he forced it out—it just wasn't feasible; he still had his in-laws' wishes to consider. But he did look forward to the party—and judging from the children's and Otto's jovial moods, they were anticipating it as much as he was.

So Levi was surprised when Otto approached him in the barn late the following afternoon wearing a solemn expression, saying he needed to speak to Levi about something awkward involving Sadie. Levi's heart drubbed his ribs. He couldn't fathom what Otto could possibly need to discuss concerning her. Did they have an argument?

For all of Otto's bluster, Levi had never seen him this bashful. "I think Sadie's a—a *wunderbaar* person," he stammered. "She's vibrant and witty and *schmaert*. And she enjoys some of the same activities I enjoy… and, well, I'd like to court her."

"*Court* her?" Levi sputtered, appalled. Realizing his knee-jerk incredulity sounded insulting, he added, "She lives in Pennsylvania. You live in Indiana."

"That's why I need your help. I thought maybe you could…I don't know, find out if she'd be open to a long-distance courtship."

Although he couldn't account for his vehemence, Levi again lost no time responding. "*Neh!* Ask her yourself."

"I can't. If she turns me down, it will be too humiliating to be in such close quarters with her until Grischtdaag."

"How will it be any less humiliating if she tells me *neh* and I tell you? You'll still have to be around her."

"I don't want you to ask her outright. Just drop some casual hints. Assess her interest. If her general response isn't enthusiastic, I won't ask her. But I'm fairly confident she'll say *jah* based on how well we get along. Plus she's been dropping some big hints lately. At least I think she has. You know how indecipherable women can be."

Levi's stomach flipped. What had Sadie said or done to make Otto think he stood a chance with her? If anyone was close to Sadie, it was Levi—he was the one who'd spent the last few weeks getting to know her during their daily lunches together. Then Levi realized he was the one who'd initiated that daily practice—he'd talked her into it. Maybe she felt obligated as his employee. Or perhaps she didn't refuse because eating separately with Levi also meant she had an opportunity to spend a few minutes alone with Otto once Elizabeth and David went down for their naps. *Neh, that's preposterous.* The more Levi tried to dismiss the possibility Sadie was interested in Otto, the more urgently he wanted to know if his brother-in-law was right.

"Okay," he agreed. "I'll talk to her."

After supper, as the children were playing in the next room and Sadie and Levi were drinking tea, she realized he'd hardly said two words all evening. She was so caught up in the giddiness of planning the get-together that she'd been rambling. "I'm sorry. I'm jumping from one subject to the next, aren't I?"

"*Neh*, it's not that." Levi a pulled a napkin across his mustache. That mustache—Sadie reminded herself not to stare. "It's that I, uh… I was talking to Otto about, uh, courtships…"

Sadie's mouth went dry, but she didn't trust herself to take a sip of hot tea without spilling it. She set down her cup and placed her trembling hands on her lap. This was what she'd been waiting and praying for, but she still couldn't believe it was happening. They hadn't even had the party yet! *For once I wasn't merely imagining a man likes me as much as I like him.* She forced herself to wait silently for Levi to continue.

Seemingly as nervous as she was, he set his cup on the table, too, twirling it in a slow circle by its handle. "Anyway…Otto was saying sometimes he'd like to court a woman but he doesn't know if she's interested. He was, ah, talking about how enigmatic women can be—"

"Ha!" Sadie uttered louder than she meant to, causing Levi to flinch. *That* was not the effect she wanted to have on him. In a quieter voice she explained, "Sometimes men are difficult to read, too. But anyway, go on."

Levi swallowed. "I—he…"

The children's voices were muffled, but Sadie recognized from their tone that an argument was about to break out. She could barely keep still. If she and Levi were interrupted, she'd fall to the floor and weep, she really would. "Sometimes it's easier to say it as fast as you can."

Levi complied. "What I'm trying to find out is if you'd be interested in a courtship. A long-distance courtship—at least until other arrangements could be made. Otto seems to think you would be and…"

Sadie's heart pranced. She just *knew* Otto could see right through her party scheme! Ordinarily she would have been mortified to learn that he'd told Levi about her interest in him, but since the revelation clearly prodded Levi to ask to be her suitor, she was thrilled. She giggled and passed her hand across her mouth. "Otto was right. I'd be very interested in a courtship."

Levi appeared absolutely dumbstruck. *He probably hasn't asked to court anyone since before he married Leora—the poor man almost looks as if he's in pain.* Sadie resisted the urge to take his hand in hers. She still wanted to hear him say the words unequivocally, not cloak them beneath Otto's suggestion. Holding her breath, she waited for him to ask her outright if he could court her.

Deceived. That was how Levi felt. He'd had absolutely no clue Sadie was interested in Otto. Not that she was required to have told Levi, but there should have been *some* indication for him to notice. Surely she would have spoken with Otto and laughed with Otto, well, the way she did with Levi. Although she and Otto got along all right, most of the time it seemed as if Sadie was doing her best to endure Otto's boorish behavior. What a facade—and Levi had fallen for it. He felt like a fool for believing *he* was the one whose company Sadie preferred, even as a friend.

As for Otto, Levi felt usurped by him. No, not usurped, but he resented the way Otto came into Levi's home and did as he pleased, whether that meant helping himself to the last piece of dessert, telling the twins he'd take them snowshoeing without asking Levi's permission or striking up a courtship with Sadie.

But Levi couldn't let on because it would have added insult to injury if Sadie knew how much it bothered him, especially when she was so jubilant. So, with as much civility as he could muster, he said, "Otto's more perceptive than I give him credit for being."

Sadie nodded. The expression on her face couldn't have been more delighted and he resented how scintillating she looked, all because of his brother-in-law. Levi's only consolation was that he hadn't acted on impulse and asked her to become the twins' permanent nanny. To think he'd even briefly considered telling the two prospective buyers, as well as his in-laws, he'd changed his mind about moving.

His in-laws! Levi was struck with the realization that if Otto and Sadie got married they'd live in the little house Otto currently owned, right down the street from his parents' house. The way he was feeling right now, Levi couldn't imagine himself attending Otto and Sadie's wedding, much less living in such close proximity to them—although David and Elizabeth would be thrilled. He shuddered and Sadie's voice brought him back to the room.

"I think a couple of mice are trying to find out what gifts they're getting for Grischtdaag," she said, a finger on her lips. Levi heard the floorboards creaking, too. The twins' shadows flickered near the door and he was glad for an excuse to change the subject.

"I'll check to see if I have an extra mousetrap," he warned loudly as he pushed his chair from the table and stood. Just then, Otto entered the house through the mudroom. Levi could hardly greet him, but of course Sadie set a place for him to have a late supper.

As she scooped *yumasetta* onto Otto's plate, she announced, "Oh, Levi, I meant to tell you that Jaala and Abram invited me to go with them to Aquilla King's *haus* tomorrow because his family is out of town and he won't have anyone to worship with. So I won't be coming over in the morning like I usually do on off-Sundays…"

Letting her sentence dangle, she caught Levi's eyes and shrugged. Was she waiting for an invitation to come over once she returned? *No way. I'm not going to make this courtship any easier for the two of them than I already have.*

Otto filled in the silence. "Don't forget, we're going snowshoeing tomorrow afternoon."

"I haven't forgotten. I'm looking forward to it." Sadie glanced in Levi's direction again.

Aha, so that's why she's giving me so many funny looks. She's hinting for me to leave so she and Otto can discuss their plans. Levi wasn't having it.

"I'm going to give the *kinner* a bath now. There's no need for you to stay and do the dishes, Sadie. Otto can clean his own plate." Levi said it politely but it wasn't thoughtfulness that prompted him to dismiss Sadie; it was a juvenile desire to cut her visit with Otto short. Admittedly, Levi was pleased when her shoulders slumped in disappointment.

"Oh, okay." She looked Levi squarely in the face. "I, um, really enjoyed our conversation tonight, Levi. As far as we got… We can, uh, talk more tomorrow."

What more did she expect him to say? She was wrong if she thought that him questioning her on his brother-in-law's behalf meant he was going to facilitate a courtship between her and Otto. The two of them weren't teenagers; they'd have to work it out themselves from now on.

Levi had barely stepped into the living room after bathing the children and putting them to bed when Otto asked, "Did you talk to Sadie?"

The answer was heavy on Levi's tongue. He was tempted to lie like nothing he'd ever been tempted to do before. He felt like he had chalk for teeth and he ran his tongue over them before admitting, "*Jah*, she said she'd be interested in a long-distance courtship."

"That's terrific!" Otto clapped Levi's back. "*Denki* for talking to her. I'm going to ask to court her tomorrow afternoon when we go snowshoeing. I have to admit, I was miffed you wouldn't let the *kinner* go snowshoeing with us, but it turns out to be a *gut* thing. Now Sadie and I will have plenty of time alone to talk."

As much as Levi regretted that decision, Elizabeth and David regretted it even more.

"I wish *we* could go snowshoeing," David griped the next day as he stood on the sofa to watch Sadie and Otto crisscrossing the yard in the snow.

"What have I told you about not climbing on the furniture, David?" Levi asked.

"I'm not climbing. I'm standing very still."

Levi didn't know if his son was talking back or was simply stating what he saw as a fact. "Get down now, please."

Elizabeth beckoned David to join her in front of the adjacent window. "You can stand next to me."

They were quiet for a while as Levi read *The Budget*, but suddenly they broke into laughter. "Sadie fell down, Daed."

Levi wasn't amused. "You shouldn't laugh when someone falls."

David reported, "But Onkel Otto tried to help her up and he tripped and fell down, too. They're covered in snow and they're laughing."

Levi had heard enough. "*Kumme* away from that window right now."

His tone must have taken them aback because Elizabeth's eyes welled and David said, "But we're safe and sound with both feet on the ground."

Since when do my children talk back to me? Levi wondered. He already knew the answer: since he'd allowed Sadie and Otto to trample over his boundaries. *All* his boundaries. He might not have any influence over Otto, but Sadie was still under Levi's employment, and as soon as Levi got the chance he was going to remind her exactly what kind of conduct he expected from her in front of the twins.

"That was such *schpass*," Sadie told Otto when they finally sat down on the porch of the *daadi haus* to remove their snowshoes. "Except my dress is wet from falling so often."

"How about I build you a *gut* fire and you fix me a mug of hot chocolate?"

Sadie hesitated. All day she'd been yearning to finish her conversation with Levi—rather, for *him* to finish it by making their courtship official—but since Otto had gone out of his way to rent snowshoes for them, it seemed rude to turn him away. So she agreed.

A few minutes later, as they were sipping their drinks in the living room, she said, "My *brieder* will be envious I got to snowshoe."

"Maybe later in the season, I'll take you cross-country skiing, too."

Later in the season? That meant Levi must have spoken to Otto about Sadie visiting Levi again after Grischtdaag. She wondered whether they'd reunite in

Maine before Levi moved, or in Indiana. Feeling self-conscious Otto knew more about her courtship—her *almost* courtship—with Levi than she did, she responded vaguely, "Well, I do have to go home for Grischtdaag, but hopefully we'll get to see each other again soon and we can go skiing then."

Otto cleared his throat. "So then, uh, you're definitely open to a long-distance courtship? I mean, I wasn't sure, which is why I suggested Levi talk to you about it first…"

Sadie bobbed her head and beamed. "*Jah*, I'm very much open to it. Just do me a favor and don't mention it to anyone, okay? It's not the kind of thing we discuss where I *kumme* from."

Otto grinned. "Don't worry. As happy as I am about it, I'll keep it a secret," he promised. "It won't be easy having a long-distance courtship, but it will only be for a short time."

Levi definitely must have spoken to Otto about when he hoped to see Sadie next. Maybe Levi would even ask her to return to Maine permanently, the way Maria suggested! She could hardly wait to talk to him and find out. Rising, she said, "I'd better put on some dry clothing now."

Otto stood, too, but he didn't leave. "I'm very happy you said *jah*," he told her. Before she knew what was happening he leaned down and kissed her cheek.

"*Absatz!*" she said, taking a step backward and swiping her hand across her cheek. She didn't care if he was the twins' uncle or Levi's brother-in-law; *that* was inappropriate and she had half a mind to dump the remainder of her hot chocolate over his head.

"I'm sorry!" he immediately apologized, red-faced.

"I thought it would be all right to begin our courtship with a kiss. I should have asked first."

"*Our* courtship? What are you talking about?" Sadie's mind was spinning.

"What am I talking about?" he repeated. "What are *you* playing at? Thirty seconds ago you very clearly said *jah*, you wanted a long-distance courtship with me. And you told Levi you did, too."

"I most certainly did not. I told Levi I'd be interested—" In a rush, Sadie comprehended what had happened. Her legs felt tottery, so she plunked herself back down onto the couch. "Otto, I'm sorry, but there's been a misunderstanding."

Otto's ears were red now, too. He closed his eyes to ask, "Then you don't want to walk out with me?"

"I'm flattered you'd ask me to but—"

"Spare me the consolation speech," Otto said bitterly. "If you weren't interested, you shouldn't have flirted with me."

Sadie was indignant. "When did I ever flirt with you?"

Otto threw his hands in the air. "That first night, in the grocery store when you said I'd be fortunate to be married to you. And the way you always tease me about rationing my food. And all that talk about pairing up at the party being more *schpass*. Not to mention, we just spent the entire afternoon snowshoeing together. *Alone*."

Sadie felt as if she was looking into a mirror of her past when she saw the bewildered hurt in Otto's eyes. *Now* she understood how such a miscommunication could occur. Now she finally believed neither Harrison nor her two suitors had intended to hurt or mislead her. They'd said as much, but until she was on the other side of the equation Sadie had doubted their veracity. She only hoped Otto would be quicker to forgive than she'd been. "I am so sorry, Otto. I know how you feel because I've been in your shoes. But I truly never meant to give you the wrong impression or hurt your feelings."

"For not trying, you did a *gut* job of it," he answered back. "You also made a fool of me in front of my brother-in-law."

"Not as big of a fool as I almost made of my*self*," Sadie muttered. She'd been so distraught about Otto's misinterpretation of her words and actions it hadn't occurred to her until just now that Levi never would have agreed to play matchmaker between Otto and her if he'd had any romantic interest in Sadie himself.

"How did you almost make a fool of yourself in front of—" Otto stopped midsentence as the meaning behind Sadie's words seemed to dawn on him. He raised his eyebrows. "*Levi?* You thought Levi was asking you about a long-distance courtship with *him*, didn't you?"

Sadie covered her face with her hands. *"Jah."*

Guffawing, Otto dropped into the chair behind him.

"It's not funny, Otto," Sadie scolded. "It's bad enough you know about it, but do you have any idea how humiliated I'm going to feel when Levi finds out?"

"Jah, I think I have an idea," Otto wryly replied and then cracked a smile. He was being so good-natured about the whole fiasco it made Sadie see a side of him she hadn't noticed before.

"I suppose what goes around comes around," she quipped. "I really am sorry, Otto, and I hope this little… misunderstanding doesn't interfere with our friendship. I think you'd make someone a terrific suitor. That was actually the reason—part of the reason anyway—I wanted to have a little party. I thought it would give you and Maria a chance to get better acquainted."

Otto rose and stoked the fire before answering with his back to her, "It's all right. I hope you don't let, ah, what I did *kumme* between us. I never would have—"

"Of course you wouldn't have," Sadie interrupted. The less said about that kiss, the better. When Otto turned to face her, she pressed her palms together. "One more thing... Could you please not mention this to Levi yet? I want to tell him myself."

Actually, she didn't want to tell Levi at all. She wanted to run away to Pennsylvania in the middle of the night.

"But he knows I was going to officially ask to court you this afternoon. Are you saying you want me to act as if we're walking out?"

"*Neh.* That wouldn't be right. But maybe you could act like we're not *not* walking out?"

"Fair enough," Otto said, grinning. "But from now on, I want a bigger portion of dessert."

Barely mumbling a few words in greeting, Otto seemed more subdued than Levi expected when he returned from snowshoeing with Sadie. Since it was past dark, Levi assumed the two of them had had supper at her house. In any case, he and the children had already eaten a typically light Sabbath meal of bologna and cheese sandwiches, and Levi was too begrudging to inform Otto there were leftovers in the fridge. Besides, Otto immediately joined Elizabeth and David in the living room, so Levi poked his head in to say he had a chore to take care of outside.

His "chore" was to talk to Sadie, who took longer

than usual to answer her door. At first Levi wondered if he'd caught her sleeping or if she had a fever. Then he realized her ruddy face and pink-rimmed eyes must have been the result of spending the afternoon outdoors. She seemed reluctant but invited him in. He followed her through the mudroom, but instead of taking a seat at the kitchen table he stood on the little braided rug near the entrance.

Levi didn't mince words. "What I have to say won't take long. I only want you to know the twins were watching you and Otto snowshoeing and when you fell, they got a kick out of it."

Sadie shrugged. "I suppose we did look comical. I was pretty clumsy in those contraptions. They take some getting used to."

"You don't understand what I'm saying. David and Elizabeth look to you as a role model. If they see you performing stunts, they'll want to try them, too. I can't stop Otto from doing whatever he's going to do, but you're my employee—for a few more days anyway—and I'd appreciate it if you set a better example for the *kinner.*"

Sadie shook her head and knitted her brows as if she thought she hadn't heard him correctly. "We weren't performing stunts, we were snowshoeing. Very slowly, I might add."

"*Jah*, and that's your business if you want to spend your Sabbath cavorting in the snow with Otto. But I'd ask that you do it out of sight from the *kinner.* They're young and impressionable. I don't want them copying your antics. They might take it too far."

"Cavorting? My *antics*?" she mocked. "You know, Levi, I actually thought you were changing, that you'd lightened up a little. But you haven't, not at all. You said it was Leora's dream to raise Elizabeth and David here. But you might as well have been living in Indiana this whole time because you've robbed the *kinner* of some of the best parts of growing up on a farm. You're keeping them from fully experiencing the joy of childhood."

"I'm keeping them *safe*." Levi distinctly pronounced each word.

"Being safe isn't the same thing as being joyful," Sadie replied. "But *jah*, you're the safest, most cautious man I've ever met."

Levi didn't care for her scornful tone but if that was her opinion of him, fine. "I don't need you to agree with my choices for the *kinner*, but I do expect you to respect them," he said before turning on his heel and exiting the house.

Chapter Nine

For the first time since arriving in Maine, Sadie had no desire to get out of bed. For one thing, if she was this cold bundled up in quilts, she couldn't imagine how freezing she'd be crossing the yard to Levi's house. For another, she was still seething over Levi's rebuke the night before and she feared the moment she saw him she'd let loose a tirade of her own.

She slipped her arm from beneath her covers to grab her pen and diary from the nightstand. Propping herself on her elbow with the quilt tucked around her, she began to write. *Every time I think it's going to be different with Levi, he resorts to his usual overbearing overprotectiveness. It's so stifling; not just for the children, but for me, too. I've been trying to be understanding of him, but he shows no understanding of me. He doesn't get it that I relish being physically active, especially outdoors, and don't mind the bumps and scrapes that come with it. The sad part is Levi has other redeeming qualities and he actually has a fun side, too—it's just so difficult to get to that I'm fed up with trying.*

As far as him worrying about me being a bad ex-

*ample for the twins? Ha! He should be more concerned
that he's teaching them to become timid little rabbits.
It's not as if the children saw me break my leg—all I
did was fall in the snow. What is there in that to make
him so angry?*

*If I didn't know better, I'd think he was jealous of
Otto for spending time with me. But to be jealous he'd
have to be romantically interested in me, which he
clearly isn't. As if I care! I don't have a whit of romantic interest in him anymore. If it weren't that the children would be so disappointed if I left early, I'd go
home right now. As it is, I'll complete my last few days
here, but it's not going to be easy to face him without
getting angry all over again.*

Fortunately, when Sadie arrived at Levi's house, Otto
said Levi had already headed to the northeast section
of trees. He indicated Sadie probably shouldn't expect
him for lunch, either. *Let him go hungerich, then,* she
thought.

"Did he reprimand you for your cavorting antics,
too?" she asked Otto.

"What do you mean? I hardly crossed paths with him
last night and when I did, he didn't have much to say.
Don't worry, your secret is safe with me."

"What secret?" Elizabeth asked from the hallway.

Before Sadie could respond, David came into the
room, announcing, "We saw you and Onkel snowshoeing, Sadie."

Right behind him, Elizabeth reported, "You fell
down six times, Sadie. I counted."

"You're right, I did fall down a lot. And even though it
hurt a little bit and I got wet, it was worth it." Sadie didn't
care what Levi said about her being a poor example, she

was going to teach the children how to be resilient if it was the last thing she did before leaving Serenity Ridge. "The important thing isn't whether or not you fall down. It's whether or not you get up and try again."

Elizabeth said, "Onkel Otto, did it hurt when *you* fell down yesterday?"

With a smirk in Sadie's direction, Otto admitted, "The big fall I took at the end of the day bruised my self-esteem a little, but the other falls I took didn't hurt."

"What's selfish steam?" Elizabeth asked, causing Otto to crack up.

"It's something inside you that makes you feel good."

"Like peanut butter sheet cake?" David asked.

Otto laughed again, but Sadie took the opportunity to say, "Speaking of peanut butter sheet cake, I'm afraid we're going to cancel our party tonight."

"Aww!" David wailed.

"How come?" Elizabeth demanded to know.

Otto revolted, too. "*Jah*, why would you cancel the party?"

Sadie was surprised he'd still want to have a party, but more to the point, *she* didn't want to have one. "I didn't think you'd, uh, still be interested."

"I'm always interested in a party, especially when there's the chance to get to know the guests better."

Aha! Otto still wants me to match him up with Maria. Sadie had to give it to him: he didn't waste any time sniveling about being rejected. "I understand, and maybe I can arrange for the guests to meet each other at another time. I'll still make the cake, though."

"But you told us we could choose a game," David protested.

Sadie was resolute. "Sometimes plans change. It's important to be a *gut* sport."

Otto gave her the eye. "*Jah*, that's true. But you also just said it's important to get back up and try again after we fall down. That's what I'd like to do."

Sadie heaved an exasperated sigh. She couldn't imagine a party being any fun with Levi there, but for Otto's sake, she gave in. "Okay, okay. We'll still have the party."

When Otto came home for lunch later in the day, Sadie asked if he'd watch the children for a minute while she ran to the *daadi haus* to get an extra sweater. For as many layers as she was already wearing, she was still chilly and she figured she'd be even colder after the twins' naps when they all went outside. Wouldn't it just figure the one day she couldn't seem to get warm, Levi wasn't around to build one of his blazing infernos in the woodstove.

The parking area was thrumming with activity and Sadie noticed someone pointing at her as she crossed the lawn on her way back to Levi's house. She kept her head down but heard the woman say, "Look, Edward, there's an Amish woman. Doesn't she look quaint in that bonnet?"

It's a prayer kapp, Sadie silently corrected her.

"I'll take a picture," Edward replied.

Sadie obscured her face as she hastened her pace. She was halfway up the path when she lost her footing. Her arms windmilled as she tried to keep her balance, but she fell backward and landed with an ungraceful thump on her backside. *Lovely. Edward probably captured that on film.* She pushed off the snow to stand but stepped on the back hem of her dress, yanking herself to the ground a second time. As she arranged the fabric so it would be clear of her boots, a shadow darkened the snow. Levi.

"Are you hurt?" He crouched in front of her.

"Neh." I wouldn't admit it if I were. "Please move so I can get up before the entire parking lot photographs me making a spectacle of myself."

"Here, let me help you," Levi offered, taking Sadie by her arm.

"I don't need help. I need you to back off!" Sadie snapped.

Levi dropped Sadie's arm like it was a hot poker. He didn't blame her for being cross; he noticed last night how slick the pathway between their two houses was and if he hadn't been so peeved then, he would have stopped to throw sand on it. As Sadie stamped toward the house, Levi went to the barn for a snow shovel and a bucket of dirt, bypassing the customers who'd been gawking at Sadie and him. One person signaled she needed help lifting a tree onto her car, but he told her Walker would be right there. Levi's priority was Sadie's safety.

The snow was packed down so Levi decided to return to the barn to retrieve the shovel he used for digging dirt. It had a sturdier blade than the snow shovel and he'd be able to crack the frozen snow into pieces in order to scoop it to the side. As he was heading toward the path a second time, Walker spotted him.

"Hey, Levi—we could use your help over here," he called.

"When I'm done," he yelled back, ignoring the line of half a dozen customers near the baling machine.

Walker's comments about not ruining relationships with his customers sprang to mind, but Levi quickly dismissed them. If the Englischers weren't going to purchase a tree because he wasn't available at the snap of their fingers, he'd accept losing the sale. *I'd rather lose money than lose my wife*, he thought before catching his error.

It wasn't Leora herself who popped into his thoughts; it was Leora's accident. He *tried* to give his guilt to the Lord, but it wasn't as easy as Sadie made it seem. He'd lived with it for so long that after a while it seemed a part of him, like a chronic illness.

Levi jammed the shovel hard into the snow. It struck the frozen earth and his hands vibrated from the force. He cleared the path right down to the ground and then he threw more dirt atop the exposed soil. There. That should keep Sadie from slipping. Maybe now the disdainful look in her eyes would vanish. For as upset as he'd been at Sadie and Otto the day before, Levi reckoned Sadie had twice as much reason to be angry with Levi now. It was hypocritical of him to have lectured her about taking unnecessary recreational risks when he hadn't properly cleared the path she used daily.

He hadn't planned to eat lunch with Sadie that afternoon, but after all that shoveling he was ravenous and he owed her an apology. For as little time as he had left with her in Maine, Levi wanted it to be harmonious.

When he went inside and found her in the living room his voice cracked with nervousness. "Hi, Sadie."

She barely glanced up from the book she was reading. "I didn't think you were eating lunch, but in the fridge there's leftover split pea soup you can heat. Biscuits are in the pantry."

"Denki," he replied, stalling. He held his hands over the woodstove. No wonder Sadie was swaddled in a quilt; the stove wasn't throwing off as much heat as usual. He added a few logs. "That should help."

"Mmm." Sadie licked her index finger to flip a page.

"Uh, can I talk to you about something?"

She snapped the book closed. "Go ahead."

Levi shifted his stance. Then he decided to take a seat on the chair opposite her. Leaning forward, he rested his hands on his knees. "I'm very sorry I didn't shovel the path better. I don't blame you for being angry, but I hope you'll forgive me."

Sadie wriggled free from the quilt and stood. "Fine, you're forgiven." She walked toward the hall.

"If you really mean that, why do you sound so angry?" His question stopped her in her tracks and she whirled around.

"Because you apologize for things that don't matter but you won't apologize for the things that do. It's as if you care more about clearing your conscience than about reconciling our relationship. You care more about your conscience than about *my* feelings." She turned and left the room.

Levi jumped to his feet and followed her to the kitchen sink, where she'd begun rinsing potatoes. He positioned himself slightly behind her left shoulder. "How have I hurt your feelings?" he asked, although he already had an inkling.

The pale nape of her slender neck was exposed as she bent forward, scrubbing the spuds. "I've taken your concerns about the *kinner* into consideration every single day. I've gone out of my way to respect your wishes, even though they often feel restrictive to me." Sadie reached into a drawer and pulled out the peeler and began slashing at the potatoes, intermittently using the back of her hand to wipe her eyes. "Yesterday was the one day I got to cut loose outdoors with another adult instead of with the *kinner*. To have *schpass* taking on a new challenge—and you tried to shame me for it. You implied I was a bad example for Elizabeth and David when I wasn't doing anything wrong."

Levi was at a loss for words. He'd never meant to make her cry and it unsettled him as much as if he'd caused her physical pain. He lifted his hand to cup her shoulder but realized she probably would flinch at his touch, so he dropped it to his side again. "Sadie, please put that down for a minute. Please?" he pleaded softly into her ear.

She dropped the potato into the sink with a thud, but she held on to the peeler and wouldn't turn to face him.

"Please, *kumme* sit," he coaxed, tugging her sleeve. She jerked her arm away in a backward circle but eventually she set the peeler on the counter and took a seat at the table.

He pulled out the chair next to her and turned it so he was facing her profile. "You're absolutely right, Sadie. You've made a lot of concessions for me. There's no one I trust more with my *kinner* than you."

She used her apron to dab at her eyes. "You have a funny way of showing it."

"I'm sorry about that. And I'm especially sorry about saying you weren't a *gut* example. You're a terrific example to the twins. And to me. I was just…"

Levi swallowed hard. How could he admit what he'd come to realize this morning after a sleepless night stewing? How could he confess he hadn't really lashed out at Sadie yesterday because she was being reckless? Nor was he volatile because he felt duped—that was part of it, but that wasn't the main reason. No, what he truly resented was that she and Otto were having such a pleasant time frolicking together—the way Levi had with Sadie before he'd put a self-imposed end to it. It burned Levi that Otto could have what Levi couldn't: a romantic relationship with a woman. And, as wrong as he was to do it, Levi had taken his envy out on Sadie, the object of Otto's affection.

Another tear rolled down her cheek. Usually so effervescent and unflappable, she appeared downright miserable, thanks to Levi. If humiliating himself was the only way she'd feel better, he'd make that sacrifice. "I was jealous," he said.

Sadie sniffed. Was it possible she'd been right about Levi wishing he could have spent Saturday alone with her? Despite what she'd written in her diary that morning about no longer having any attraction to him, her heart fluttered with new hope. "Jealous of what?"

"Otto, mostly."

"Why?" This time, she wasn't jumping to any conclusions. She was going to make him spell it out.

Levi sat up straight and cleared his throat. "Probably because the two of you were having such a *gut* time and… I think I was jealous of your freedom. Especially Otto's. He's always been more daring than I am."

So it *didn't* have anything to do with Levi liking her; it was about a rivalry between him and Otto. Sadie blew the air from her cheeks, deflated. At least this time her hopes were dashed quickly. As reluctant as she was to encourage Levi to continue when his words were so distressing to her, she knew she owed it to him as a friend to be supportive. There was nothing wrong with what he was saying—it just wasn't what she was hoping to hear. "You can have that kind of freedom, too, Levi. It's yours for the taking. But you can't hold on to guilt and experience freedom at the same time. You have to make a choice."

"I know. And I'm trying to choose freedom. I've asked the Lord to help me. But letting go doesn't come as easily as I thought it would."

"I understand," Sadie conceded, because she did. As often as she had tried to change, here she was, back at square one, longing for a courtship with someone who didn't reciprocate her interest. "I try to be patient—"

"You've been very patient," Levi confirmed. "Far more patient than anyone else has been or would be and I appreciate it more than I've shown. If you'll give me another chance, I'll change."

Knowing from her own experience how often she'd needed another chance, Sadie couldn't hold a grudge against Levi. "Of course I'll give you another chance. Now, how about if you go wash up and I'll serve us both some lunch?" Although she hadn't intended to eat with him, she had been too upset to eat earlier and now that they'd cleared the air, she was starving.

After she fixed their bowls and they said grace, Levi remarked, "The *kinner* are going to miss you a lot. But who knows, if things work out between you and Otto, maybe we'll get to see you again in Indiana."

Sadie held a biscuit in the air, midway to her mouth. She didn't want to tell Levi about her misunderstanding—it was so humiliating. But she couldn't allow him to think she was interested in Otto. Especially since they were still having the party and it would be obvious when she paired Otto up with Maria for the games. "Otto and I aren't walking out together."

Levi's spoon slipped from his grip and clattered into his bowl, spraying broth. He wiped the table before asking, "You aren't? But you told me the other day you'd be interested—"

"He and I talked it over and...we decided we aren't the right person for each other," Sadie said more truthfully than not.

Levi's eyes were huge. "Wow."

"Wow, what?" Sadie questioned, affronted. "I didn't intend to mislead him or to hurt his feelings. I'd never do that on purpose."

"*Neh*, of course you wouldn't. It's just that it must have been a hard blow for him to bear. If I were in his place, I feel pretty dejected."

If you were in his place, I would have said jah. "Fortunately for him, Otto bounces back quickly," Sadie said.

"*Jah*, he's resilient as well as intrepid."

Hearing the wistfulness in Levi's voice, Sadie encouraged him, "There's nothing Otto can do that *you* can't do, if you put your mind to it."

Levi looked down at his interlaced fingers. "There is *one* thing," he muttered.

"What's that?"

"He can... He can ask a woman to walk out with him."

Sadie inhaled sharply. Was Levi speaking hypothetically, or was there someone he wanted to walk out with in particular? *I can't imagine who that would be, but then again, I had no idea Harrison was interested in someone from another district,* she reminded herself. Then she wondered, *Is it* narrish *to think maybe* I'm *the one he wants to court?* If so, what would make Levi believe he couldn't ask her, especially now he knew she and Otto weren't walking out?

"There's nothing stopping you from asking to court a woman, either," she hinted.

"*Neh.* I had my chance," he said, pushing his hair back.

Sadie gently replied, "I think Gott gives us more than one chance at most things in life, especially when they involve something as virtuous as love."

"*Jah,* well…" Levi got up and rinsed his plate in the sink without finishing his sentence.

Realizing she wasn't going to get any further on the subject right now, Sadie asked, "If I tell you a secret, will you promise not to let on?"

That captured Levi's attention again. He turned and faced her. "I promise."

"I intend to match up Otto and Maria at the party."

"Ah, *gut* idea. I'll try to keep the twins from thwarting your efforts." Levi chuckled. Then he brought up a subject he'd never directly broached with her before. "You must miss being home and going to parties at this time of year. I've always wondered why you'd choose to *kumme* here during Grischtdaag season."

Sadie was still too embarrassed to tell him about Harrison and how she'd quit her job. "I could say I was trying to help out *familye,* but since we're not related and you're only a distant relative of Cevilla's, I can't keep making that claim. So let's just say I needed a change of scenery."

Levi pulled on his beard. "Now that you've had a change of scenery, are you ready to go home?"

"I suppose I am," she said. *There's not much point in staying here.*

"The *kinner* will miss you."

"I'll miss them, too." *And I'll miss you.* "But once they're settled in Indiana with your in-laws, they'll forget all about me."

"I doubt that's true."

"Oh, it is. Time and distance have a way of doing that, and that's as it should be. They're young, they'll meet a lot of people in their lives, but no one will ever be as important to them as the people they live with every day."

You're *the one I want in our daily lives.* The longing flashed through Levi's mind with an intensity that startled him. *That's* lecherich. *I couldn't possibly ask Sadie to stay after she practically said the* kinner *and I are forgettable and she wants to go back to Pennsylvania. And I owe it to Leora's folks to include them in raising Elizabeth and David.* So instead of asking her to stay with them in Maine, Levi repeated his thanks for Sadie's patience and promised to relax about the children's safety rules.

She stopped collecting their dirty dishes to smile at him. "I'm glad to hear that, because I'm going Grischtdaag shopping tomorrow night with Maria and I plan to buy Elizabeth and David a zip-line kit. You didn't seem too keen on my *brieder*'s clothesline-and-pulley invention, but I figure you won't object if I purchase a real zip line for you to install."

Levi gulped before he realized she was kidding. He'd

miss her kidding. "As long as it's sturdy enough to hold me, too," he teased back.

Sadie giggled. "Seriously, though, I'd like to get them each a sled. You have great hills around here."

"That's very generous of you." He was going to show her he meant what he said about lightening up about his rules for them. "They'd love to go sledding."

Although Levi was relieved he'd made up with Sadie, their discussion about her leaving kept him from feeling truly content. For the rest of the afternoon, he ruminated on her response to his question about going back to Pennsylvania. She'd only said she *supposed* she was ready to return. That wasn't the same as saying she couldn't wait to go home. Maybe there was still a possibility she'd consider staying in Maine as Elizabeth and David's permanent nanny. And if she would, maybe there was a way he could smooth things over with his in-laws…

He was so preoccupied he didn't notice Otto approaching him in the parking lot after Levi helped the last customer ease a tree into the back of her van and she drove away.

"Do you mind if I go in now?" Otto asked. "I, uh, want to take a shower before supper tonight."

Levi fought a smile; Otto wanted to impress Maria. He had to give it to the guy—Otto was eternally optimistic, just like his sister had been. And, in some ways, like Levi had been before Leora's accident. "Go ahead. Walker will help me put away the equipment and I'll do the milking. By that time, Maria should have the cash box reconciled and ready for me to look over."

Usually Levi saved the milking for his final task before coming inside, but in a gesture of generosity—

or maybe it was guilt over being so sore at his brother-in-law—he figured he'd delay Maria in order to give Otto more time to prepare himself. Otherwise, knowing Otto, he'd damage his chances with Maria by showing up to supper still dripping wet.

"I was starting to think you went to the party without me," Maria said when Levi entered the workshop half an hour later.

"*Neh*, Sadie wouldn't have let me in the door without you. Neither would the *kinner*."

Levi briskly double-checked the figures in the ledger; once again, the day's sales exceeded his expectations. As he walked toward the house with Maria, the milk pail in his hand, Levi commented he was surprised people were still purchasing trees and wreaths this late in the season.

"Some folks wait until the last minute," Maria said. "Which is a shame, since they could have been enjoying the beauty of a tree for weeks before now. Everyone has their reasons for putting things off, I suppose."

Because it was dark, Levi couldn't see her expression, but he had a niggling feeling Maria wasn't referring to procrastinating customers. He pointed at the windows. "Look, Sadie must have lit the candles."

"Aw." Maria paused to admire them. "She's brightened all our lives, hasn't she?"

Now Levi was certain Maria was up to her matchmaking tricks. This wasn't the first time she'd tried to set him up with someone, but it was the first time he didn't mind. Or wouldn't have minded, if Sadie lived in Serenity Ridge permanently. *What am I thinking? Asking to court Sadie would be even more* lecherich *than asking her to stay in Maine...* Chalking the wayward idea up to Maria's influence, Levi shifted the milk pail to his other hand and continued with her toward the house.

They had barely ascended the first step when the door flew open. David and Elizabeth hopped up and down, unable to contain themselves.

"*Wilkom*, Maria," Elizabeth called and nudged David, who ran onto the porch in his stocking feet.

"May I take your coat?" he asked.

Levi's heart swelled; he recognized Sadie's influence on the twins' manners. "That's very kind, David, but let Maria *kumme* into the house first, okay?"

The twins backed through the door, but they kept talking as David hung Maria's coat on a low peg and Levi untied the laces of his boots. When he opened the door from the mudroom leading to the kitchen, a fragrant aroma filled his nostrils.

"Did you see the candles from outside, Daed?" Elizabeth asked.

"You said an adult could light them for a special occasion," David reminded Levi before he could answer.

Sadie turned from the stove. Backlit by the candlelight, she appeared to be aglow. "Hello, Maria. Hi, Levi. I hope you don't mind that I lit them." She gestured toward the window, but Levi couldn't tear his gaze away from her face.

"I don't mind at all," Levi said. "Everything looks beautiful. Absolutely lovely."

And I wish everything could stay this way. But as David pointed out, this was a special occasion. After Christmas, everything would change.

Sadie's legs felt weak from the way Levi was looking at her. Her yearning to be in a courtship with him had crept back into her heart the minute after he returned to work that afternoon, and his compliment now only encouraged her fanciful thinking. *Don't be* narrish, she told herself. *He's referring to the decorations—to the candlelight and the place settings—not to you.*

"Hi, Maria." Otto came into the kitchen. Before his shower Sadie had informed him she'd told Levi that she and Otto weren't walking out. Now that Otto was free to openly express an interest in getting to know Maria, he apparently wasn't wasting any time.

"As soon as you wash up, we can eat," Sadie said to Levi.

"Onkel Otto already washed up. He took a shower," Elizabeth reported to Maria, causing Sadie to cringe. Fortunately, Maria only laughed and Otto seemed unfazed.

"Would you like to sit here?" Otto pulled a chair out for Maria.

"That's *my* seat," David protested. "I always sit next to you, Onkel Otto."

"*Ach!* I forgot." Otto smacked his forehead, not appearing at all chagrined to have his preference exposed.

"How about if I sit across from you instead, Otto?" Maria asked. If Sadie wasn't mistaken, she was batting her lashes.

Elizabeth took Maria's hand and led her to the table. "*Jah*, it's better if you sit next to me, Maria. Onkel Otto takes almost all the mashed potatoes before he passes them."

"Elizabeth, that's not polite," Sadie scolded, but the child couldn't hear her over Maria and Otto's laughter. It was clear the pair wasn't going to need any matchmaking help from Sadie. Sadie wasn't sure if she was impressed or envious; Otto didn't seem the least bit embarrassed to be seen clearly vying for Maria's attention. *How many times have I wished a man would be that blatant about wanting to get to know me better?*

After supper everyone enjoyed a large slice of peanut butter sheet cake, followed by a card game Elizabeth suggested and a round of charades David wanted to play. Then Levi announced it was bedtime for the twins. Sadie immediately said she'd clean up in the kitchen and adamantly refused any help from Maria—she wanted to allow Otto and Maria an opportunity to visit alone in the living room.

When Levi returned, Sadie was placing teacups on a tray.

"You blew out the candles," he observed.

"Safety trumps romance," Sadie ribbed him, only half joking. "Besides, Otto and Maria don't need romantic lighting—they seem to be getting along just fine."

"*Jah.* I'm surprised they didn't notice each other before tonight."

"Sometimes people miss the most obvious opportunities for love," Sadie replied wistfully, knowing her hint fell on deaf ears.

Lifting the tray, she walked into the other room without giving Levi a backward glance. Which, unfortunately, was probably how she'd have to leave Serenity Ridge in a few days, too.

Chapter Ten

Since Sadie and Maria had made arrangements to go to the mall on Tuesday right after the tree lot closed, Sadie prepared supper for Levi, Otto and the children before she left.

"You didn't have to do that," Levi said. "We would have managed."

"Speak for yourself," Otto contradicted him. "What are we going to do when Sadie leaves in a couple of days?"

"I don't know about the rest of us but you're probably going to lose weight," Levi needled his brother-in-law.

Sadie forced a chuckle even though Levi's light-hearted response disappointed her. Clearly her departure was going to be harder on her than it was on him. *What did I expect?* she scolded herself. But no amount of self-recrimination kept her from clinging to the tiniest shred of hope.

As she was leaving, Otto followed her into the mud-room. "I, uh, wanted to say *denki* for matching me up with Maria last night. We had a great time."

"I'm glad." Sadie was no longer surprised he'd be so

open about a topic Amish men didn't usually discuss; that was just the way Otto was.

"*Jah.* She and I have a lot more in common than you and I do. You turning me down as a suitor may have been the best thing that ever happened to me."

"Otto!" Sadie was indignant. She hadn't wanted him for a suitor, but there was no need to point out how relieved he was she'd refused him.

He turned red. "*Ach!* I didn't mean to sound insulting. I meant Maria might be the woman the Lord has intended for me for all these years and if you hadn't rejected my offer of courtship, I wouldn't have considered walking out with her."

"Isn't it a little early to tell if she's the Lord's intended for you?"

"Perhaps, but I think when you know, you know. Don't you?"

Neh. *I've* always *thought I'd found Gott's intended for me, only to be proved wrong, three times in a row. Four, if I count Levi.* Rather than sharing any of that, Sadie simply replied, "I'm glad you're enjoying getting better acquainted."

She'd barely boarded the buggy before Maria was shaking her finger at her. "After all the grief you gave me for helping Grace set you up with Jonathan, I should be ticked off at you for pairing me up with Otto last night."

Sadie giggled. "You said *should* be ticked off. But you aren't. That must mean you enjoyed getting to know Otto better?"

"*Jah.* And when we were talking about how cold it is, I mentioned one of my windows at home has a terrible draft and he offered to *kumme* over tomorrow night and repair it. So I invited him to stay for supper, too."

That means he won't be with Levi, the kinner *and me for our little* "familye" *celebration,* Sadie realized happily. "In that case, you'd better stop at the supermarket tonight, too. That man eats more than anyone I know—and I have seven *brieder*!"

Maria chuckled before hinting, "When you invited me to your get-together, I actually thought the party might be a facade so you could spend time with Levi in a social setting without the *kinner*."

"Hmm." Sadie's murmur was noncommittal.

"C'mon, I told you how I felt about Otto. Be honest. You like Levi, don't you?"

Sadie sighed. "*Jah,* I do—you can't tell anyone I said that, though. Not that it matters. Levi hasn't expressed any romantic interest in me."

Maria clicked her tongue. "You'd make a terrific couple. But you know how cautious Levi is. Maybe he likes you, but he's afraid. Maybe he's working up to expressing himself."

"I've been telling myself the same thing, but sooner or later I'm going to have to accept the truth. He's simply not interested in me like that. Besides, I'm leaving in two days."

"There's still time," Maria insisted. "He could still ask to be your suitor."

"He could also decide to ski down Mount Katahdin, but I don't think that's going to happen, either."

Suddenly, Sadie was struck with an idea of what to get Levi for Grischtdaag—a gift card to rent snowshoes. She'd write something on it like "Here's to taking a step toward freedom." When she told Maria about the snowshoes, Maria deftly halted the horse and reversed their direction so Sadie could purchase the gift card before the rental shop closed.

Afterward, they continued to the mall, where Sadie bought a red sled for Elizabeth and a blue one for David. Even though the shop featuring all-Maine products was touristy, Sadie wanted to buy her family's gifts there, since it would probably be her only time visiting the state. She purchased a Maine-shaped cutting board for Cevilla, wool socks for her father, an assortment of wooden toys and puzzles for the younger boys and fishing nets for her older brothers. She nearly squealed when she found a solid "chocolate moose"—the perfect gift for Otto. And for Maria she purchased a small leather diary. *She can fill it with reflections on her courtship with Otto*, Sadie thought plaintively. *I hope it turns out better than any of* my *relationships with men.*

Levi stood in the middle of the aisle of the outdoor-gear-and-apparel shop holding a pair of new work gloves he intended to purchase for Otto, who'd recently torn his. Levi had purchased Elizabeth's and David's gifts— a doll and a handmade wooden tractor and wagon—at a local craft fair last summer, so now the only gift left to choose was Sadie's and he had no idea what to get her.

"What should I buy for Sadie?" he asked his children.

"A new coat," Elizabeth answered. "So she can stay outside longer."

David disagreed. "Remember when I asked if she was too cold in her skinny coat and she said *neh*, she was tough?"

Levi chuckled; that sounded like Sadie, all right. Actually, a thicker coat was a great idea; it was something he'd wanted to get for her ever since the first snowfall. But a gift like that would be inappropriate. The Amish didn't usually exchange large gifts at Christmas, focusing instead on celebrating the birth of the Savior, and Levi was concerned she'd feel overwhelmed if he bought her an expensive present. Not to mention, it was the kind of gift a man gave to a woman he was courting, which was obviously not the case with Levi and Sadie. So he and the children continued wandering through the store, considering other options.

"How about a pair of snowshoes? You can get Onkel a pair, too and then they can go snowshoeing again," David suggested.

"I already decided on these gloves for Onkel Otto."

"Besides, Sadie is going home the day after tomorrow," Elizabeth scolded.

"You don't know everything, Elizabeth. Daed might ask her to stay."

Levi set down the gloves and squatted beside David. "What makes you think that?"

"You said at the *hochzich* that you might ask her to stay, 'member?"

"I'm pretty sure Sadie needs to get home to her *familye* now."

David persisted. "But did you *ask* her to stay?"

"Neh." He rose and reached for a pair of protective shoe and boot coverings on the shelf beside him, asking, "What do you think of these? They're called crampons. You wear them over your shoes so you don't slip on the snow or ice. Sadie could use these in Pennsylvania."

David wasn't to be distracted. "Why not, Daed? Why didn't you even ask her?"

This wasn't how he wanted to tell his children they'd

be moving, but Levi was trapped. He explained, "I've been thinking that after Grischtdaag, you, Elizabeth and I should move to Indiana. We could live with Grooss-mammi and Groossdaadi. Onkel Otto lives nearby, too. So, you see, there would be no reason for Sadie to stay in Maine. You won't need a nanny anymore. Grooss-mammi will take care of you in Indiana. Ant Hannah will help, too."

"I don't want to live in Indiana," whimpered Elizabeth.

"Me, neither." David's eyes were welling.

"Hush," Levi said sternly, not only because *Englisch* customers were looking at them, but because he felt emotional himself. He whispered, "Groossmammi and Groossdaadi can't wait to spend more time with you. Their feelings will be hurt if we don't go live with them."

"Can't they *kumme* to our tree farm?" David asked.

"*Jah*, they could stay in the *daadi haus* and Sadie could *kumme* live in our *haus*. She can share my room with me," Elizabeth offered.

"Sadie isn't staying in Maine and neither are we. I don't want to hear another word about it." Levi stood up, tucked the gloves and crampons beneath his arm and took each of his children by the hand.

After paying for the gifts Levi hurried the twins to the buggy. On the way home the children were so quiet Levi thought they'd fallen asleep in the back of the carriage, but when they got into the house he saw their noses and faces were raw from crying and once again he had to bite his lip to keep his own feelings in check. This Christmas was not shaping up to be the happy occasion Levi hoped to provide for them. He felt so disheartened after he put Elizabeth and David to bed he retreated to his bedroom and flopped on the bed fully clothed, his mind awhirl.

Within minutes Walker's horse clopped up the driveway, bringing Otto home—because of the late evenings they put in, all of Levi's staff members were forced to do their holiday shopping at the last minute. Levi could hear the low, muffled hum of his brother-in-law singing as he opened and closed the kitchen cupboards, no doubt rummaging for something to eat. Although Levi couldn't hear the words, he immediately recognized the joyfulness of the tune for what it was; the song of a man who had the hope of a new courtship. The sound ate away at him. Levi pictured Otto marrying Maria and moving to Maine. Whereas Levi...Levi was moving back to Indiana, into his in-laws' home, a regression of sorts—certainly not what Leora wanted for their family. Not what Levi or the children wanted, either.

Then just as distinctly as a cupboard door snapping shut, an idea clicked in Levi's mind: it was still in his power to *try* to change their situation. Hadn't Sadie encouraged him to put his mind to the things he really wanted to do? He could at least *ask* her to stay on as the twins' nanny. If she said yes, he'd find a way to work it out with his in-laws and the potential buyers, but there was no sense in worrying about those details until he consulted Sadie, first. He sprang to his feet and hurried to the kitchen.

"I'll be back in a little bit," he told Otto as he pushed open the door to the mudroom. His brother-in-law's mouth was full, but Levi didn't wait for a response.

He flew across the lawn beneath the moonlight, so intent on his mission he didn't realize until he'd knocked several times there were no lights on in Sadie's house. Mindful she might have turned in early, he knocked louder; he'd rather wake her than wait another instant to ask her to stay.

After rapping his knuckles sore, Levi became convinced Sadie hadn't returned from shopping yet and he resigned himself to watching for the buggy from his porch. He was halfway back to his house when he realized the baler had been left outside. *Whose turn was it to put it away? Mine? Otto's?* Figuring it was an easy enough task to overlook in their urgency to go shopping, Levi rolled it into the barn. While he was there he added another blanket to the horse—it was going to be another frigid night.

As he started back toward the house, he spotted a large lump on the ground near the opposite side of the parking area. It was…yes, it was a baled tree. How had it gotten so far from where the other cut and baled trees were leaning against the wooden frame? Levi wondered if it could have rolled off the roof of a customer's car without someone noticing it. *Or could this be the work of vandals?* He heaved it onto his shoulder to carry to the barn. If it really did roll off someone's car, they'd come looking for it tomorrow and he wanted it to be ready for them.

The Frasier fir was heavier than he anticipated and he was attempting to get a better grip on it when he heard the crunch of footsteps behind him. Already on high alert, he swung around to see who was following him.

"Yow!" a woman shrieked and Levi staggered before setting the tree down. He could barely see her form sprawled on the ground, but he recognized the voice as Sadie's.

* * *

"Sadie!" Levi exclaimed. "You're hurt, aren't you?"

Stunned, Sadie held her breath, trying not to cry. Aware of Levi's tendency to overreact, she attempted to assure him she was okay but only a moan came out. Before she realized what was happening, he wrapped one arm around her torso and slid his other arm beneath her knees. She protested weakly, but he didn't listen, so she clasped her hands behind his neck and rested her head against his shoulder as he straightened his posture. This was *not* how Sadie had envisioned them embracing, and even in the midst of her pain, she felt cheated. Levi barged across the yard and up the porch, and then Sadie felt his stance shift and his muscles tighten as he raised his foot to kick the door.

Otto opened it and Sadie squinted from the glare of the light. "What happened? Is she okay?"

"I knocked her down." Levi carried Sadie into the living room and gingerly eased her from his arms into a reclining position on the sofa. Kneeling beside her, he asked if she thought she'd lost consciousness.

Sadie noticed how his face had gone pale and how there was a look of desperation in his eyes. He was so close to her she could see the individual whiskers of his mustache. Most were dark but some were reddish and a few even bordered on being blond. She had studied his mustache a hundred times and never noticed the variations in color until now.

Levi's lips were moving. "Sadie, did you hear me? Did you lose consciousness when the tree hit you?"

Wondering whether she felt dazed because of Levi's proximity or from her injury, she replied, "*Neh*. It surprised me but didn't knock me out."

Elizabeth and David shuffled into the room, disheveled from sleep. "What happened?"

Instead of answering, Levi told Sadie, "To be on the safe side, we should take you to the hospital."

Elizabeth burst into tears. "Is Sadie going to die, Daed?"

"I don't want you to die." David wrapped his arms around Sadie's lower legs.

Irritated she had to calm everyone down when she felt so crummy herself, Sadie stated firmly, "I'm not going to die and I'm not going to the hospital, either." Then she directed Levi to bring her a warm, wet cloth, Otto to fill a dishcloth with snow, Elizabeth to get a glass of water and David to bring her a pillow from upstairs.

Her uncharacteristically demanding tone did the trick; everyone stopped fussing and swiftly carried out her requests. After dabbing the warm cloth against her skin where baling string or pine needles had scraped her face, Sadie gently pressed the cloth-bound snow to her cheek. The others hovered around her until she said, "Quit staring at me like that, please. I'm fine."

The twins backed away and settled onto the oversize chair while Otto stoked the fire, but Levi remained crouched beside the sofa. His coloring was better now, but his expression was still laden with remorse as he scrutinized her. *If only he was as sorrowful about my leaving as he is about my injury... If only he knew what's* really *hurting me...*

"You may feel okay now, Sadie," he said. "But we should make sure you don't have a concussion. I twirled around really fast. The force might have—"

"Pah!" Sadie sputtered. "I don't have a concussion.

The tree didn't hit me that hard. Even in the dark I saw it coming out of the corner of my eye. I was already starting to duck."

"All the same, I think—"

"*I* think it's time for the *kinner* to get back to bed. Do you want to take them or should I?" Sadie figured threatening to walk upstairs in her condition was the only way she could get Levi to stop harping about going to the hospital.

"I'll do it," he said glumly before leading the children away.

"I'm glad Sadie's not going to die," Elizabeth said.

Levi recognized the question in his daughter's statement; she needed reassurance. He was the last person qualified to give it to her, but he said, "I'm glad she's going to be fine, too."

"So am I," David agreed. "I love her."

"I love her more than you do," Elizabeth challenged him.

"You do not," David countered and their arguing was music to Levi's ears, a return to normalcy.

After tucking them in, he padded down the stairs and into the living room. Sadie was alone, sitting upright, but her eyes were closed and she rested her head against the pillow David had brought her. *She's so pretty.* Immediately Levi felt a pinch of guilt for having such a thought, especially now, when Sadie was wounded. Because of him. He cleared his throat and she opened her eyes.

Sitting across from her, Levi listened as she explained how she'd asked Maria to drop her off at the end of the driveway. In case the twins were awake, Sadie didn't want them to hear the horse and look out the window because she was carrying—actually, pulling—their Christmas gifts. She had just stashed the sleds in the barn and was going to the *daadi haus* when she saw someone carrying a tree up ahead of her. Uncertain whether it was Otto, Levi or a thief, she was sneaking up behind him to get a better look.

Levi gasped. "That was dangerous! If it had been a thief, there's no telling what might have happened." It was an ironic thing to say, considering he'd just clocked her in the head with a tree.

"I was fairly certain it was Otto or you. Although I couldn't make sense of why you'd be hauling trees at this time of night."

"I wasn't. I'd actually gone to the *daadi haus* to talk to you about something when I noticed a stray tree in the parking lot. I thought we had vandals. That's why I spun around like that. I'm so sorry."

"It's my fault. I was following you too closely and it was dark. I must have startled you."

It was true, she *had* startled him, but that didn't make Levi feel any better about what he'd done. *How could I have been so* dopplich? he chastised himself, just as he'd done following Leora's accident. Flooded by memories and stricken by feelings of shame and inadequacy, Levi could hardly speak and was glad when Otto reentered the living room.

"I just put the spare tree in the barn, Levi," he said, warming his hands near the stove. "I hid the sleds, too, Sadie."

"*Denki.* Perhaps tomorrow before supper you could bring them to the porch, Levi, so I can give them to the twins when we're done eating?" She shifted on the cushion, allowing both men a better view of her swollen cheek. Poor Sadie—she was probably in more pain than she was letting on.

Otto whistled. "You're going to have some shiner in the morning."

"I haven't had a black eye since my *bruder* spiked a volleyball at me. Now, *that* was no accident. But it turned out well for me because he had to do my chores for a month," she said.

"I wouldn't want to eat Levi's cooking for a month." Otto guffawed. "Your *eldre* are going to take one look at you and regret ever letting you *kumme* to Maine. I'd love to see their faces when you tell them Levi whacked you with a Grischtdaag tree."

"Maybe I should say I got bowled over by a moose, instead." Sadie started to smile but then she cringed and touched the side of her face.

Levi recognized Otto was only kidding, but his words cut him to the quick because they were true. Sadie's family—and Sadie herself—had entrusted her welfare to him as her employer. And through carelessness, he'd proven himself incapable of taking as good care of her as *she'd* taken of him and his children. Which was the same that could have been said about him and Leora…

His self-reproach was interrupted when Sadie rose and slipped the quilt from her shoulders and folded it into a square. "I should go."

Levi was relieved when she didn't refuse his offer to walk her to the *daadi haus*. After seeing her inside and building a fire in the woodstove, he asked, "Can I get you anything else?"

"*Denki*, I've got everything I need. But you never

said what it was you were coming to talk to me about before you hit—before I fell."

Levi hesitated. Beneath the glare of the kitchen's overhead gas lamp, Sadie's cheek looked even worse than it had before and a line of red tracks was forming where she'd been scratched by pine needles. *I did that to her.* The desire to erase the damage, to soothe away her pain with a thousand gentle kisses was so intense Levi's legs trembled. *What am I thinking?*

Levi couldn't ask Sadie now—maybe he couldn't ask her at all. He needed more time to decide.

"It can wait. Let's talk about it tomorrow evening, after the *kinner* go to bed." In the event he didn't ask her, he figured he'd be able to come up with another topic by then.

At home Levi found Otto standing by the kitchen sink polishing off the last piece of peanut butter sheet cake. "You know, this cake reminds me of Leora. She frequently made it because she knew how much I like it," he said in between bites. "I still miss her a lot. I miss her sense of humor, her courage. The way she always looked on the bright side of things."

"I still miss those things about Leora, too."

"Don't get me wrong, I love both my sisters, but Hannah's not like Leora was." Otto wiped his sleeve over his lips. "Leora's more like…like Sadie—"

"Leora was one of a kind—"

Otto held his hands up and halted Levi midobjection. "Of course she was. But her *temperament* was more similar to Sadie's than it is to Hannah's."

Between the twins' meltdown and Sadie's injury, Levi had little patience left over for Otto's rambling, especially about Leora. "Just what are you getting at?"

"I think if Leora had to choose someone to care for Elizabeth and David, she'd choose Sadie over Hannah and my *mamm*. And I think you owe it to Leora to choose Sadie, too."

Levi balked. "But—but I don't even know if Sadie would be willing to stay here for *gut*."

"That's right, you don't. You've got to take a chance—take a *risk*—and ask her first." Otto clapped the crumbs off his hands and left the room without another word.

Levi slumped into a chair. Was Otto right? Resting his head on the table, he covered his head with his hands, as if that could keep his mind from reeling. Round and round his mind went until sheer exhaustion forced him to come to a conclusion: *Elizabeth and David need Sadie. They* love *her. Just because I've been an irresponsible employer doesn't mean* they *should suffer. And I'll try even harder to be careful from now on...* Yes, for his children's sake, Levi was still going to ask Sadie to stay on as their permanent nanny.

The night seemed to go on forever. It wasn't pain that kept Sadie tossing and turning—not physical pain anyway. It was the excruciating desire to know what Levi wanted to talk to her about. When morning finally arrived, Sadie discovered Otto was right; she definitely had the start of a shiner. Or half a shiner. The bruising on her swollen cheek—deeper red today, with a hint of blue undertones—was creeping sideways toward her eye, but at least the scrapes were crusted over.

"How do you feel?" Levi asked before she even crossed the threshold of the mudroom into the kitchen.

"I'm *gut*." Relatively speaking.

"Sadie, your face looks like this," Elizabeth informed her, puffing out one of her own chubby cheeks. Sadie had to giggle; it was a case of the kettle calling the pot black.

She and the twins occupied their morning with baking, cleaning and singing, followed by a late-afternoon trip to the workshop. Since the van would arrive to pick Sadie up at eight o'clock the next morning and the farm was closed on Christmas Eve, Sadie wanted to take the opportunity to bid Maria goodbye. The women exchanged gifts, promising each they wouldn't open them until the twenty-fifth.

"Levi hasn't asked you to stay…or asked you anything else?" Maria whispered into Sadie's ear as they embraced.

"Neh." Sadie didn't mention Levi wanted to speak with her later. There was no sense disappointing Maria if things didn't work out as she hoped—Sadie would be disappointed enough for both of them.

Maria pulled her head back and looked her squarely in the eye. "There's still time."

"You're going to keep saying that until the moment my van drives away, aren't you?"

"Jah. Unless Levi professes his undying love before then, in which case I'll say I told you so!" Maria said, making Sadie crack up.

Buoyed by Maria's optimism, Sadie herded the twins home so she could prepare a pot roast. Any sadness the children felt about Sadie's departure was overshadowed by their anticipation of exchanging gifts, and supper was a lively, talkative occasion. Elizabeth and David were so excited they didn't even want to eat the bread pudding they'd helped Sadie make for dessert.

The four of them gathered in the living room to read the Nativity story from Scripture, pray and sing a few carols. Then Levi told the children it would be nice if they gave Sadie her gifts before opening their own. David shyly presented her with a small cardboard box. Inside were a dozen oddly cut pieces of wood.

"It's a puzzle. I drew it and Onkel Otto cut it out. It's a tree. A Fraser fir."

"Now open mine," Elizabeth demanded, giving Sadie a sachet of balsam potpourri made from needles she'd collected herself.

On the brink of tears, Sadie could hardly get the words out. "*Denki.* I'll treasure these." She wrapped her arms around both of them. When she finally let them go, she clapped her hands. "Now, time for your gifts!"

After telling the children their presents were too big to wrap, she asked them to close their eyes until she brought in the sleds from where Levi had rested them against the house on the porch.

"Okay, you may open your eyes now," she said.

"Sleds!" David whooped.

"One for each of us!" Elizabeth hollered. "Daed, can we keep them?"

"Of course you can keep them," Levi answered, although Elizabeth's uncertainty wasn't lost on Sadie. She wondered if Levi would resort to his usual restrictions after she left.

"Can we go sledding tonight?"

"*Neh*, not in the dark," Levi said.

"How about if we go tomorrow morning, bright and early, before I leave?" Sadie asked.

"That's a *gut* idea. Elizabeth and David, you'll need

to get some sleep so you can be up and dressed by the time Sadie comes over in the morning," Levi suggested.

The children obligingly scrambled upstairs, lugging their plastic sleds into their rooms with them. Levi got them ready for bed while Sadie prepared tea and dessert, which she brought into the living room. When Levi returned, he took a seat in the chair and Sadie handed him his cup before sitting on the sofa. She was so intent on finding out what he wanted to talk to her about, she couldn't swallow a morsel of bread pudding and she would have forgotten entirely about exchanging gifts with him if he hadn't handed her a box wrapped in bright green paper and tied with a gold bow. With trembling hands she pulled the paper off, revealing a photo of some kind of funny footwear.

"Snowshoes!" she exclaimed. Otto had said snowshoes came in various shapes and styles and it delighted Sadie that Levi gave her a gift that appealed to her fondness for athletics.

"Er, *neh*. They're protective foot coverings. Crampons. You put them on over your boots and they keep you from slipping," Levi explained.

Sadie's mood plummeted and her eyes burned. *It's the thought that counts*, she told herself. Which was exactly why she felt so let down. Even Harrison had given her a more personal present than that. Blinking, she managed to utter her thanks before handing Levi the envelope containing the gift card she gotten him.

His mustache widened with a smile when he read the inscription aloud. "*Denki*. I'll enjoy using this sometime in the near future... And speaking of the future, there is, uh, something I'd like to ask you to consider."

The future? With those two words, Sadie's disappointment over the crampons was entirely forgotten. As Levi took a long pull of tea, she drew her spine up and clasped her hands on her lap, bracing herself for what she knew—this time she was *sure*—he'd say next. He was going to ask her to stay in Serenity Ridge.

"Since you seem to like our little community here, and since the twins are so fond of you, I was wondering if—if you'd, er, be willing to return to Serenity Ridge after Grischtdaag to continue as their nanny. Indefinitely, I mean. That way, we wouldn't have to return to Indiana. You do such a *wunderbaar* job I can't imagine anyone, even my in-laws, taking such *gut* care of Elizabeth and David."

"Denki," Sadie mumbled even though she didn't feel especially complimented. Was that really all she was to Levi—a superior babysitter? He'd said the twins were fond of her, but he hadn't uttered a single word about how *he* felt about her. Not even that he thought of her as a friend. She'd been hoping and praying for so long that he would ask her to stay, she thought once he finally did, she'd be ecstatic, but she just felt numb.

"I realize it's a big decision," Levi acknowledged when Sadie didn't say anything else. "I haven't told the twins or anyone else I was going to ask you, so you can take your time to decide. Maybe let me know before January 1?"

"You're right. I do need time to consider it. January 1 is fine," she replied. "For now, it's getting late. I'd better turn in so I can go sledding in the morning like I promised the twins."

When she got home she snuggled into bed a final time, pulled out her diary and wrote.

Tonight Levi asked me to return to Maine perma-

nently—as a nanny. After wanting it for so long, I really thought I would have leaped at the opportunity to stay here indefinitely. I thought it was exactly what I wanted—or at least, it was the next best thing. And maybe it is. Maybe if I stay, Levi will develop the same kind of feelings for me that I have for him, and he'll work up the courage to ask to be my suitor...

Or am I just repeating my mistake of holding on to false hope, of seeing what I want to see? If I return to Serenity Ridge to become the twins' permanent nanny, a year from now will I look back and regret all the time I spent loving someone who doesn't love me back and never will?

Chapter Eleven

"What's all this?" Sadie asked as she entered Levi's kitchen a little before seven o'clock the next morning.

"We wanted you to enjoy a hearty breakfast that you didn't have to prepare yourself," Levi said. The French toast had actually been Elizabeth's idea—she'd helped Sadie prepare it several times before and was delighted to walk Levi through the steps. Otto had made eggs and perfectly crisp bacon and David had peeled oranges and placed the sections into a bowl for everyone to share.

Sadie's smile, always effulgent, was especially dazzling today. Not even the purpling of the skin beneath her eye and along her cheek detracted from her mirthful expression as she thanked them.

"Daed didn't even burn the French toast."

"Not yet I didn't, but we'd better sit down and say grace before I do," Levi suggested. After everyone was seated, they bowed their heads and Levi prayed, "Gott, *denki* for this food. We ask You to bless our bodies with it. *Denki* for Sadie's presence here and her willingness to help us and to serve You. Please give her a safe trip back to Pennsylvania. We ask these things in Jesus's name—amen."

As he was serving breakfast, Levi was struck by the realization that today might be the last time he ever saw Sadie and the lump in his throat kept him from enjoying the thick, sweet, golden French toast and fluffy scrambled eggs. The children, however, devoured their food in no time flat, clearly in a rush to go sledding.

"I'll wash the dishes later," Levi suggested when Otto and Sadie finished eating. He wanted the twins to be able to spend as much time with Sadie as they could before she left. Since Otto was on his way to Maria's house to weatherize a couple more windows, before they went outdoors Sadie brought in a gift bag from the mudroom for him. In turn, Otto presented her with a box tied with red ribbon to open on Grischtdaag.

"So, I guess this is goodbye. It's been *schpass* getting to know you. *Denki*, Sadie, for…you know, for everything," Otto said and Levi assumed his comment was in reference to the matchmaking she did between him and Maria.

"*Denki* for teaching me how to snowshoe. I'm so glad we were here at the same time," she replied, giving him a quick hug from the side.

I wonder if I'll *get a hug goodbye, too.* The unbidden thought quickened Levi's pulse before he could dispel it from his mind. He was going to have to do better at banishing those thoughts if Sadie accepted his offer of employment.

"Have a *gut* time sledding," Otto said. He was out the door and on his way to Maria's before Sadie and Levi could get themselves and the twins bundled into their coats.

"Be careful not to trip over my suitcase—I left it on the porch so I could go sledding up until the time the van comes," Sadie warned as they stepped outside. Right as she was speaking, a vehicle turned into the driveway.

"Oh, *neh*! Is that your driver already?" Elizabeth whimpered.

"I don't think so…"

The minivan parked near the workshop and an elderly couple slowly got out and came toward them. Levi was tempted to tell them the tree lot was closed—it was after all—but when they apologized profusely, saying they hadn't bought a tree earlier because they didn't think their grandson would be discharged from the hospital in time for Christmas, Levi couldn't turn them away. He reluctantly told Sadie and the children they should start sledding without him. Then he fetched a handsaw and led the couple to the balsam firs, knowing they wouldn't have enough strength to cut and transport the tree back to their vehicle themselves.

After they finally selected a tree and Levi baled it and loaded it into the back seat of their large van, he feared it was close to eight o'clock. He figured Sadie and the twins would have been sledding on the hill in between his house and the *daadi haus*, but since they weren't in sight he wondered if they'd already gone back inside.

"Aaaaaah!" In the distance Elizabeth released a bloodcurdling scream.

"Aaaaaah!" David echoed.

Their cries were coming from behind the stand of pine trees on the other side of the barn, where the larger hill was located—the hill with the *pond* at its base! Terrified, Levi tore off in that direction, nearly losing his footing twice on the slippery snow. His heart walloped his ribs as the icy air ripped his breath from his lungs, but he didn't slow his pace until he pushed aside the pine branches and burst through to the clearing.

His momentum carried him forward several steps even after he spotted Sadie, David and Elizabeth slowly picking their way back up the hill, chatting and laughing, pulling their sleds behind them. It took a moment for his mind to comprehend what his eyes were seeing. *They're okay. They're all okay. They're fine.* They'd been screaming because they were euphoric, not because they'd crashed through the ice or something else tragic happened.

No sooner was his panic allayed than anger overtook him. *What was Sadie thinking to bring them here?* Fully stopped, Levi bent over, his hands on his knees, trying to catch his breath and temper himself from yelling something to Sadie in front of the children he might regret.

"Look, there's Daed!" David hollered. "Daed, we're going to have a race. *Buwe* against *meed.* You get to ride on my sled with me."

"*Neh*, it's almost eight o'clock," Levis shouted back. "We have to go back to the *haus* so Sadie doesn't miss the driver."

"Just one more time?"

"I said *neh*!" Levi barked. Sadie, David and Elizabeth simultaneously snapped their heads upward to look at him, obviously taken aback by his tone. No matter how peeved he was that he'd suffered such an unnecessary fright, Levi didn't want to ruin the children's last day with Sadie, or their own Christmas Eve, either. In a softer voice he added, "Sadie and I can pull you back to the house on your sleds. We'll race—*buwe* against *meed.*"

Levi was already spent from sprinting across the acreage, so Sadie easily could have beaten him, but he sensed she allowed him to catch up in order to avoid an argument between the children. They reached the porch at the same time. After proclaiming the race a tie, Levi instructed David and Elizabeth to say goodbye to Sadie and then go inside and put on drier clothes so he could talk to her in private.

"Goodbye, Sadie." Elizabeth hugged Sadie's waist.

"I love you," David said, enveloping her from the opposite direction.

"I love you more than he does," Elizabeth tipped her face upward; tears dribbling over the mounds of her cheeks.

David tightened his grip. "No, she doesn't."

Sadie wiggled free so she could crouch down and encircle them snugly into her arms. "I think you both love me the same amount. And I love you both the same amount. Which is a whole bunch."

After they'd embraced a few moments, Levi said, "Okay, *kinner*, that's enough. Let Sadie go and I'll be in to make hot chocolate in a minute."

As she watched Elizabeth and David enter the house with their chins tucked to their chests, it took every ounce of Sadie's willpower to refrain from saying, "Don't cry. I'll be back soon."

But the truth was, after a long, sleepless night of prayer and contemplation, she wasn't sure she *would* be back; she still needed more time to think it over. As bad as she felt to see the twins so forlorn, she'd feel even worse if she told Elizabeth and David she'd come back and then changed her mind.

The door had barely clicked shut behind the twins when Levi cupped her elbow and briskly led her toward the other end of the porch.

"Why on earth were you sledding behind the barn?"

"What do you mean?" Sadie couldn't comprehend why his eyes—his kind, beautiful green eyes—blazed with hostility. "You said we should go on without you."

He pointed to the small hill between his house and the *daadi haus.* "*That's* where I thought you'd take the *kinner* sledding. *Not* down the big hill on the other side of the barn."

Ah, their old, familiar dissension. Sadie thought Levi had come to trust her judgment regarding the children's care, but clearly he still had his reservations. As indignant as she felt, Sadie kept her voice low and her tone neutral. "First of all, Levi, you didn't specify any areas that were off-limits. Second, the reason I took them to the big hill is it's actually *safer* there because there's nothing at the bottom to crash into—unlike here, where they could run into the fence. Or the house."

Levi's nostrils flared like a horse with colic's. "There's a *pond* at the bottom of the big hill!"

"A pond?" It took Sadie a moment to remember. "Oh, *jah.* I forgot about that because it's covered in snow."

"You *forgot*? How could you *forget* you were sledding over a pond?"

Sadie's tolerance was wearing thin. "If the weather had been warmer, I would have been more conscientious about what we were sledding over. But considering how many days we've had in a row of temperatures in the single digits, any water in this area has to be frozen solid. Besides, didn't you tell me the so-called pond is only four or five feet deep?"

"If someone broke through the ice, they could get hypothermia as easily in four feet of water as in twelve."

Sadie snickered. "Your milk cow wouldn't break through that ice, much less one of us."

"You're missing the point! It's one thing if you want to take risks like that when you're around Otto or your *brieder*, but it's another thing to behave so irresponsibly when you're caring for small *kinner* like Elizabeth and David!"

That was the last straw. Sadie suddenly had all the clarity she needed to make her decision. Contrary to her rash decision to quit her job at Harrison's family's store, this time walking away from the employment opportunity was completely rational. It was *inevitable*, even. But that didn't make it any less painful.

The van came rumbling up the driveway; Sadie would have to be quick. She could hardly look in Levi's direction and her chin quivered as she spoke. "No matter how fond I am of the *kinner*, I won't be coming back to Maine. I've tried but I can't continue to have the same disagreement with you again and again and again. I understand you think you're being responsible or protective or whatever, Levi. But the way I see it, you're trying so hard to keep the people you care about from being injured or dying that you're preventing them from *living*. I respect that you have to do what you think is necessary for Elizabeth and David, but your fears are too prohibitive for me."

Levi spit out his response. "Only a tomboy would think I'm too prohibitive!"

"I'd rather be a tomboy like me than a scaredy-cat like you!" Sadie hissed back at him.

She sounded like an eight-year-old even to her own ears, but Sadie didn't care. All that mattered to her was getting away from Levi Swarey as fast as she could. Her vision blurred by tears, she nearly stumbled over her suitcase as she moved toward the stairs. Without glancing toward the window to see if David and Elizabeth were waving to her, she picked up her bag and hurried toward the van.

Levi and the children couldn't have had an unhappier Christmas Eve if they tried—and from the twins' constant squabbling, he suspected they *were* trying. Not that they needed any help making Levi miserable; his confrontation with Sadie perturbed him enough to last a lifetime. If she *really* respected his concerns about the twins' safety she wouldn't have taken them sledding over the pond in the first place. Nor would she have called him a scaredy-cat when he pointed out she'd potentially put the three of them in jeopardy. Yet she'd somehow had the nerve to say *she* couldn't continue having the same argument with *him*! Levi couldn't stop replaying their altercation in his mind and his brooding resulted in a daylong headache, followed by several hours of insomnia once he went to bed. *If Sadie still thinks my guidelines for the* kinner*'s safety are so objectionable, we're all better-off without her,* he concluded as he finally dropped off to sleep.

After such a gloomy Christmas Eve, he figured Christmas Day would have to be a more festive occasion, but he woke to the children bickering in the hallway. They managed to behave themselves during their Christmas worship time as a family, which Levi imagined was because they knew they'd receive gifts afterward, but the presents only temporarily perked them up. By lunchtime, they were glum and listless again.

"I don't want noodles for Grischtdaag," Elizabeth complained. "That's what we had for Thanksgiving."

Levi figured his daughter wasn't truly upset about the food—she was upset because the food reminded her of Sadie. But that couldn't be helped. They'd already eaten the leftovers from the last meal they shared with Sadie, as well as the casserole Maria had sent home with Otto yesterday. *Why didn't I prepare better?* Levi asked himself, already knowing the answer: for several months after his mother died, either his church district regularly brought him meals, or he and the children ate frozen foods and sandwiches. Once Sadie arrived, the meals from his neighbors had stopped coming and he'd gotten so used to relying on her to cook he hadn't given much thought to taking over the task again.

"What do you want instead? Cereal? Eggs?" Levi asked.

"*Neh.* I want to take a nap." It wasn't like Elizabeth to forgo a meal or volunteer to go to bed.

"Okay. David, you should take a nap, too." Levi assumed they were out of sorts because they missed Sadie, but maybe they hadn't gotten a good night's rest. "When you wake up, we can have hot chocolate and sing Grischtdaag carols."

"I'll play charades," Otto volunteered from the sofa, where he was reading a book Maria had given him about recreational activities on nearby Mount Katahdin. "We can light the candles."

"*Neh*, we're only allowed to light them on special occasions," David refuted.

"It *is* a special occasion. It's Grischtdaag," Levi reminded him. *A time when* wunderbaar *things happen.*

David was too busy gathering the pretend wooden logs for his tractor's wagon to respond, so Levi led Elizabeth to her room first.

"What are you going to name your *bobbel*?" Levi asked when he tucked her in.

"Sadie," Elizabeth said without a moment's hesitation. She clutched the doll in her arm and rolled over, but not before Levi noticed the tear dripping down her cheek.

When Levi went into David's room, he discovered his son had brought his sled inside without Levi knowing it. David was stretched out on the floor in it with a pillow beneath his head and a blanket pulled up to his chin. His eyes were squeezed shut; clearly he was only pretending to be asleep, but Levi decided to wait until later to tell him he'd have to take the sled back outside onto the porch.

This is going to be harder than I thought. If it was this difficult for the twins to adjust to Sadie leaving, Levi didn't know how he'd ever help them transition to living with his in-laws, especially since they could be rather austere. Preoccupied with thoughts of contacting the Realtor after Christmas, Levi was descending the stairs when he stepped down on something hard and round that rolled beneath his heel. As his right leg flew out straight in front of him, he grabbed for the railing to break his fall. Although he managed to avoid landing on his backside, he came down at an odd angle on his left foot.

"Argh!" he hollered as he was gripped with excruciating pain.

Otto instantly appeared below him and Elizabeth's and David's footsteps sounded at the top of the stairs.

"What happened?" Otto asked.

"I think I slipped on one of David's toy logs," he replied through gritted teeth. "Help me into the living room, would you?"

Levi slung his arm around Otto's shoulder and used the railing on the other side to support himself. Hopping on one foot, he made his way to the sofa. Having followed them, the children watched intently as Levi slowly brought his leg up to rest on the coffee table and carefully peeled back his sock.

"It's already swelling. I'll get some ice." Otto was gone and back in a flash with a dish towel he'd filled with snow, just as he'd done for Sadie. Levi placed it on the tender skin.

"You think it's broken?" Otto asked.

"Neh," Levi replied although he wasn't sure. "I think it if was broken it would look misshapen. This is only swollen."

"Do you think you should get it checked out at the hospital?"

Hearing Otto's question, David fled the room and Elizabeth burst into tears. "Are you going to die, Daed?"

"Neh. I'm not going to die. But I probably do need to see a doctor."

"At the hospital?" Elizabeth asked.

"In the emergency room, *jah,"* Levi replied honestly. The throbbing in his ankle was intensifying. "I'm not sure how I'll get into the buggy, though."

"I'll go to the phone shanty and call Scott. He'll give you a ride in his truck."

"On Grischtdaag?" Levi questioned, but Otto was already out the door. Elizabeth was still crying, so Levi distracted her by asking for a glass of water. "And tell your brother to *kumme* join us, please."

When Elizabeth returned, she was balancing a glass filled to the brim. "David isn't in the kitchen."

"Then run upstairs and get him. I want to tell him about my trip to the hospital."

"Can we *kumme*?"

"*Neh*, I'd like you to stay with Onkel Otto."

When Elizabeth left again Levi set the glass aside—he was in too much pain to drink the water, but for the children's sake, he couldn't let on. Elizabeth tromped back down the stairs in a matter of seconds, announcing David wasn't in his room, either.

"David!" Levi called, figuring he was in one of the downstairs bedrooms or the basement. "David, this is no time for games. *Kumme* here!" He repeated himself, but when his son didn't answer, Levi directed Elizabeth, "Quick, put your coat on and stop Onkel from leaving! Run!"

Elizabeth did as she was told, but she must have left the mudroom and kitchen doors open, because Levi felt an initial burst of icy air followed by a steady cold draft, and he could clearly hear her calling Otto in the distance.

Moments later, Otto rushed inside and searched the house. Even though he'd just been in the barn and hadn't seen David, he rechecked it and searched around the workshop, too, but David wasn't anywhere to be found.

"Why would he have left the house? Where could

he have gone?" The anguish Levi felt in his ankle was nothing compared to the roiling in his stomach.

"Every time it's his turn to choose where to play, he says section D," Elizabeth informed her father.

"Section D?"

"*Jah*, on the map you gave Sadie. He likes it because his name starts with *D*. I'll show you."

That's just like Sadie—teaching the twins how to read a map and spell their names at the same time, Levi thought as Elizabeth disappeared into the kitchen and came back holding the large square of paper. She pointed to David's favorite rows within section D and Otto charged out of the house.

Levi suggested they pray, so he and Elizabeth bowed their heads together until they heard footsteps on the porch. If Levi wasn't mistaken, it was the sound of only one person approaching. His heart plummeted. *Please, Gott. Please.*

Otto came into the room carrying David, who wasn't wearing a coat or a hat and mittens. His face and ears were bright pink and he was shaking uncontrollably.

"Give him to me." Levi stretched out his arms. Otto carefully placed the boy on his father's lap and covered him with a quilt.

"I'm s-sorry, Daed." David sucked in little gasps of air. "I should have p-picked up all my toys. I'm sorry, Daed. I don't want you to d-d-die."

"It's okay, David. It's okay," Levi repeated. "It was an accident. I should have been watching where I was walking. I know you didn't mean for me to get hurt."

Levi rubbed David's arms and rocked him the way he hadn't done since he was a toddler, both of them in tears.

* * *

The day after Christmas, Sadie's church district observed Second Christmas, a day for the Amish to visit and exchange small gifts with their extended families and friends. But between her contentious departure from Levi, the long trip home, fielding endless questions about what happened to her cheek and her younger brothers' excitement over Christmas, Sadie was exhausted. So, much to Cevilla's dismay, when the rest of the family was getting ready to journey to her eldest brother's home on the other side of town, Sadie excused herself from accompanying them.

Once everyone left, she retreated to her room. There she set her suitcase on a chair. She had rummaged through it to retrieve the gifts for her family members the day before but otherwise hadn't unpacked it yet. When she lifted a folded apron, she uncovered a small box—she'd forgotten all about it, but recognized it as the gift from Maria. Inside was a small battery-operated clock, its face decorated by a sweet little painting of a blueberry bush. Sadie knew the clock was meant to emphasize Maria's oft-repeated encouragement "There's still time."

Not anymore there isn't, Sadie thought, uncovering a second box. Otto's gift was a mug with a black bear painted on it. She thought of him looking for a black bear dessert in the grocery store, which made her crack up. But suddenly her laughter turned into sobs and she couldn't stop crying.

After all the tears she'd shed into her pillow the last two nights, Sadie would have thought she'd cried herself out, but apparently she hadn't. For as firmly as she believed she'd made the right decision in telling Levi she wasn't returning to Maine, Sadie still cared about him and the twins. She still missed them, and it had only been two days. Even though she knew it wasn't good for her to wallow in her sorrow or cling to her memories, she decided to read her diary. *I might not have a future with Levi and his family, but at least I have a past.*

She had just curled up on the sofa with hot chocolate in the mug from Otto and was leafing through her diary when there was a knock at the door. With a sigh, she set the diary aside, lifted the quilt from her lap—now that she was so acclimated to Maine's temperatures, the quilt was unnecessary anyway—and reluctantly went to answer it. What she saw on the porch shocked her. Levi was propped up on two crutches and wearing a medical walking boot. Levi. *In Pennsylvania.*

"*Frehlicher Grischtdaag,*" he said.

Her concern for his condition temporarily overshadowed any misgivings. "Are you okay?" she asked, neglecting to wish him a merry Christmas, too.

"It's only a sprain. A bad one, but no broken bones." The strain in his voice indicated he was worse off than he claimed.

"What happened?" Sadie was so stunned to see him there and in such a condition she didn't invite him inside the house.

"I slipped on David's toy and landed on my ankle wrong."

"I'm so sorry to hear that." And she was, but she couldn't concentrate on his injury when there was a more pressing question on her mind. "Why have you *kumme* here?"

"I want to talk to you about something important, but, uh, it's kind of difficult for me to keep standing here."

Still on the defensive, Sadie joined him on the porch. "All right, have a seat." She ambled to the swing and held it steady so Levi could situate himself. Then she leaned against the rail opposite, facing him, her arms crossed over her chest. She wasn't cold; she was leery.

His voice fraught with remorse, he elaborated on the story of how he'd been injured, focusing on the aftermath when David had felt so guilty he ran from the house without a coat to his favorite section of the farm.

Picturing the little boy shivering in the cold, Sadie's eyes filled and she pressed her hand flat against her heart to quiet it. "You must have been terrified when you couldn't find him."

"*Jah*. And when I realized *why* he had run away—" Levi's eyes watered, too. "I was devastated to see my son racked with guilt like that. And then it really sank in. I finally got it, that Leora wouldn't want me to feel guilty about her accident, either."

"That's true." Sadie nodded, but she didn't see what any of this had to do with her.

"I wasn't to blame for Leora's accident, but I am to blame for how unfairly I treated you after you took the *kinner* sledding. You're right, Sadie—I have a tendency to apologize for things I don't need to apologize for, but not for the things I should. So I'm apologizing now. I'm very sorry I treated you so unfairly and unkindly—and I hope you'll forgive me."

Sadie only hesitated a split second. Forgiving Levi came naturally. She liked him so much, and besides, the Lord knew how many times *she* needed to ask for forgiveness. "*Jah*, I forgive you, Levi. And I probably could have been…more tactful in how I responded to your concern about the *kinner*. I realized later you probably heard the twins screaming and you didn't know it was from sheer exhilaration."

"I wasn't just frightened on the *kinner*'s behalf, Sadie. When I heard their screams, I was frightened something had happened to *you*. I don't think I could bear it if…" Levi's voice drifted off but there was no need for him to complete his thought; Sadie understood.

He looked so solemn she waited a moment before jesting, "Well, nothing *did* happen. As I've told you, we tomboys are tough."

For the first time since she'd opened the door, a shadow of a smile crossed Levi's face before they both burst out laughing. It felt like old times again. When they quieted, Levi asked, "Could you please get that box the driver left over there?" He pointed to a large white box at the bottom of the porch stairs, which was sitting next to a knapsack. Sadie hadn't noticed it earlier. She brought it to him, but he shook his head and told her it was for her.

Sadie didn't want a gift. She'd already forgiven Levi; he didn't need to do anything else to show her how sorry he was. "Levi—"

"Please, just open it."

Sadie reluctantly balanced the box on the railing and lifted the lid to find a dark blue woolen coat. She held it up in front of her. It appeared warm and well made and the color was distinctly feminine. When she tried to tell him she couldn't accept it, Levi cut her off.

"It's the gift I've wanted to give you for weeks. But I didn't want to overwhelm you with something so personal. And I still felt guilty about Leora's death. My guilt made me feel like I didn't deserve to…to feel toward any woman the way I feel toward you. Or to hope you feel the same way about me."

Sadie's thoughts were churning. So, her perception was accurate; Levi *had* been drawn to her romantically. But whatever glee she experienced to hear him admit he liked her was dashed by the reality that she and Levi were too different to have a harmonious relationship. It just wouldn't work.

In the face of Sadie's silence, Levi continued, "So that's the gift I should have given you. And the question I should have asked was if I could court you. It would be *wunderbaar* if you'd return to Maine to continue caring for Elizabeth and David, too, but I'd understand if you'd prefer a long-distance courtship. That's completely up to you. All that matters to me is that you allow me to be your suitor."

Although it shredded her heart to refuse him, Sadie knew she couldn't say yes. "You don't for how long or how much I've wanted you to ask me that, Levi, because I do share similar feelings for you. But we can't walk out together. We're too different. We've both tried to adapt to each other's expectations and it hasn't worked."

"You don't need to adapt to my expectations anymore, Sadie. *I'm* the one who has to change. I've said that before but this time it's different. Don't you see? I left the *kinner* alone with Otto. He probably has them snowboarding down Mount Katahdin as we speak! I never would have allowed him to watch Elizabeth and David alone before. But I'm doing it now because I've already changed. And because you're worth taking the risk. I like you so much, Sadie."

In all of the times Sadie ever imagined what it would be like to have a man make it abundantly apparent how much he cared for her, she couldn't have dreamed up anything that moved her as much as what Levi just said. She was speechless—no, she was *breathless*—from sheer elation.

He must have taken her lack of response as indecision, because he prompted, "You were the one who reminded me Gott gives us more than one chance, especially at something as virtuous as love. Will you give me another chance, too? Please?"

Her legs wobbly, Sadie lowered herself onto the swing next to Levi and peered into his earnest, expectant eyes. "*Jah*, of course I will! I very much want to have you as my suitor and I'd love to return to Maine to be the twins' nanny."

Levi's expression suddenly came to life; Sadie had never seen him grin like that before and it made her shiver. He reached over to take the coat she'd forgotten she was still holding. "You're cold. Put this on."

He held it up for her as she stood and slid her arms into it. Sitting down again, she angled herself to face him. "*Denki*. It's so warm and pretty."

"So are your eyes." Levi leaned closer and Sadie closed her lids and tilted her chin upward to receive his kiss.

As his soft, eager mouth met hers, his whiskers feathered her lip. Sadie abruptly pulled back and giggled.

Levi's eyes sprang open. "What's *voll schpass*?"

Dismayed, Sadie clasped his forearm to emphasize her contrition. "I'm so sorry, Levi. I wasn't laughing at you. It's just that I've never kissed a man with a mustache before. It tickled."

"Ah." Levi smoothed the hair on his upper lip with his fingertip. "I'll shave it off."

"*Neh*, please don't. It looks very handsome on you."

"*Denki*, but I'm not sure my pride can take it if you pull away and laugh every time we kiss. And I, uh, I hope to kiss you a lot during our courtship."

"I won't giggle anymore. I promise."

"Really?"

"If you give me another chance, I'll prove it," she teased.

So Levi kissed her again and when she neither laughed nor pulled away, he murmured, "I guess you're right. You're already getting used to it..." Then he kissed her two more times just to be sure.

Sadie finally knew what it was like to kiss a man with a mustache and when she described it later in her diary, *perfect* was the word that came to mind.

Epilogue

Thirteen months later

"What do you think, *kinner*, are you ready to snowshoe up a mountain?" Levi called to the twins.

"Jah," David said. "I'll show you!"

"Me, too!" Elizabeth echoed.

Using their poles for balance, the children slowly but skillfully began traversing the slope on the other side of the barn, one shoulder angled toward the top of the hill, one toward the bottom, just as their uncle had taught them.

"I'm not sure *I'm* ready," Maria admitted, struggling to keep up with her new husband and niece and nephew. She and Otto had gotten married two weeks before Christmas, which was two weeks after Sadie and Levi were wedded, and the six of them had gone snowshoeing almost every Sunday afternoon since the first snowfall that season. "I never should have given Otto a book about Mount Katahdin last Grischtdaag."

Hearing her, Otto laughed and waited until she caught up with him. Not far behind, Levi and Sadie deliberately paused to watch David and Elizabeth progress toward the top of the hill.

"Their skills have really improved since last winter, thanks to Otto's instruction and all the time you spent practicing with them," Levi remarked.

"You've gotten pretty *gut* yourself," Sadie replied.

"*Denki*. I never would have made it this far without you to challenge and help me over the past year."

"Oh, I don't know about that. Otto is a very good teacher."

Levi's voice went low and serious. "I'm not just talking about snowshoeing. I'm talking about how much you've encouraged me to live a fuller life. To worry less and trust Gott more."

"My life is fuller because of you, too, Levi," Sadie replied. "So is my heart."

Levi planted his poles in the snow so he could reach over, wrap her in his arms and give her a kiss. Nuzzling his nose against her cold cheek, he whispered, "Do you have any idea how much I love you?"

"*Jah*, I do because you show me all the time." Sadie kissed her husband back. "But there's nothing as *wunderbaar* as hearing you say it in plain language."

* * * * *

Watch for the next book in
Carrie Lighte's Amish of Serenity Ridge miniseries,
coming in Spring 2020!

Dear Reader,

As someone who frequently vacations in Maine, I'm delighted to begin a new series set in the Pine Tree State. For research, my sister and I recently took a trip to the small Amish community in Unity. We enjoyed the beautiful scenery, spent time talking to a local farming family and shopped at an Amish market that sold the tallest and sturdiest clothes-drying racks we've ever seen (an essential household item if you have a large family but no electric clothes dryer). We can't wait to go back again this year; we plan to visit on a Wednesday or Saturday, which is when you can buy fresh, homemade doughnuts.

As different as *Englisch* practices and values can be from Amish traditions and beliefs, there are many commonalities, too. As you read Sadie and Levi's love story, it's my hope you'll connect with their struggles and joys, as well as get a glimpse of what it might be like to live as an Amish person in Maine.

Blessings,
Carrie Lighte

WE HOPE YOU ENJOYED THIS BOOK!

Love Inspired®

New beginnings. Happy endings.
Discover uplifting inspirational
romance.

Look for six new Love Inspired
books available every month,
wherever books are sold!

"You won't have to stay on our account, and we can look after Ernest's place, too. I can hire a man to help me. Someone I know I can..." Ruth's words trailed away.

Trust? Depend on? Was that what Ruth was going to say? She didn't want him around. She couldn't have made it any clearer. Maybe it had been a mistake to think he could patch things up between them, but he wasn't willing to give up after only one day. Ruth was nothing if not stubborn, but he could be stubborn, too.

Owen leaned back and chuckled.

"What's so funny?"

"I'm here until Ernest returns, Ruth. You can't get rid of me with a few well-placed insults."

She huffed and turned her back to him. "I didn't insult you."

"Ah, but you wanted to. I'd like to talk about my plans in the morning."

Ruth nodded. "You know my feelings, but I agree we both need to sleep on it."

Owen picked up his coat and hat, and left for his uncle's farm. The wind was blowing harder and the snow was piling up in growing drifts. It wasn't a fit night out for man nor beast. As if to prove his point, he found Meeka, Ernest's big guard dog, lying across the corner of the porch out of the wind. Instead of coming out to greet him, she whined repeatedly.

He opened the door of the house. "Come in for a bit." She didn't get up. Something was wrong. Was she hurt? He walked toward her. She sat up and growled low in her throat. She had never done that to him before. "Are you sick, girl?"

She looked back at something in the corner and whined softly. Over the wind he heard what sounded like a sobbing child. "What have you got there, Meeka? Let me see."

He came closer. There was a child in an Amish bonnet and bulky winter coat trying to bury herself beneath Meeka's thick fur. Where had she come from? Why was she here? He looked around. Where were her parents?

Don't miss
The Hope *by Patricia Davids,*
available now wherever
HQN™ books and ebooks are sold.

HQNBooks.com

PHPDEXP1219

It couldn't be.

Ice filled Ashley Willis's veins despite the spring
sunshine streaming through the living room windows of
the Bristle Township home in Colorado where she rented
a bedroom.

Disbelief cemented her feet to the floor, her gaze
riveted to the horrific images on the television screen.

Flames shot out of the two-story building she'd hoped
never to see again. Its once bright red awnings were now
singed black and the magnificent stained glass windows
depicting the image of an angry bull were no more.

She knew that place intimately.

The same place that haunted her nightmares.

The newscaster's words assaulted her. She grabbed on
to the back of the faded floral couch for support.

"In a fiery inferno, the posh Burbank restaurant The
Matador was consumed by a raging fire in the wee hours
of the morning. Firefighters are working diligently to
douse the flames. So far there have been no fatalities.
However, there has been one critical injury."

Ashley's heart thumped painfully in her chest, reminding her to breathe. Concern for her friend Gregor, the man who had safely spirited her away from the Los Angeles area one frightening night a year and a half ago when she'd witnessed her boss, Maksim Sokolov, kill a man, thrummed through her. She had to know what happened. She had to know if Gregor was the one injured.

She had to know if this had anything to do with her.

"Mrs. Marsh," Ashley called out. "Would you mind if I use your cell phone?"

Her landlady, a widow in her mideighties, appeared in the archway between the living room and kitchen. Her hot-pink tracksuit hung on her stooped shoulders, but it was her bright smile that always tugged at Ashley's heart. The woman was a spitfire, with her blue-gray hair and her kind green eyes behind thick spectacles.

"Of course, dear. It's in my purse." She pointed to the black satchel on the dining room table. "Though you know, as I keep saying, you should get your own cell phone. It's not safe for a young lady to be walking around without any means of calling for help."

They had been over this ground before. Ashley didn't want anything attached to her name.

Or rather, her assumed identity—Jane Thompson.

Don't miss
Secret Mountain Hideout *by Terri Reed,*
available January 2020 wherever
Love Inspired Suspense books and ebooks are sold.

LoveInspired.com

.